Critical Praise fo[r]
TALES OF THE OU[T]

- Winner of a PEN/Beyond Mar[gins]
- A *New York Times* Editors' Choi[ce]
- An *Essence* Magazine Best Seller

"As this new collection of short fiction (most of it previously unpublished) makes clear, the writer formerly known as Le-Roi Jones possesses an outtelligence of a high order. Baraka is such a provocateur, so skilled at prodding his perceived enemies (who are legion) in their tender underbellies, that it becomes easy to overlook that he is first and foremost a writer . . . He writes crisp, punchy sentences and has a fine ear for dialogue . . . In his prose as in his poetry, Baraka is at his best as a lyrical prophet of despair who transfigures his contentious racial and political views into a transcendent, 'outtelligent' clarity." —NEW YORK TIMES BOOK REVIEW

"A marvelously vital and creative mind at work."
—LIBRARY JOURNAL

"Baraka remains a prodigiously skilled writer. *Tales of the Out & the Gone* is an apt reminder of Baraka's unique ability to touch on politics, race, and identity in a biting vernacular style." —TIME OUT NEW YORK

"In his signature politically piercing and poetic staccato style, Baraka offers a perspective on social and political changes and a fresh view of the possibilities that language presents in exploring human passions . . . Fans and newcomers alike will appreciate Baraka's breadth of political perspective and passion for storytelling." —BOOKLIST

Tales

Tales

BY
AMIRI BARAKA

AKASHICLASSICS: RENEGADE REPRINT SERIES
BROOKLYN

Published by Akashic Books
©1967 by LeRoi Jones/Amiri Baraka; ©2016 by Amina Baraka

Originally published in 1967 by Grove Press/Evergreen Black Cat. In addition, a number of these stories previously appeared in *Evergreen Review, Pa'lante, The Moderns, Transatlantic Review,* and *Yugen.*

Cover photograph by Carl Van Vechten and used by permission of the Van Vechten Trust.

ISBN: 978-1-61775-395-4
Library of Congress Control Number: 2015934073

Akashic Books
Twitter: @AkashicBooks
Facebook: AkashicBooks
E-mail: info@akashicbooks.com
Website: www.akashicbooks.com

Contents

Tales

A Chase
(Alighieri's Dream)

Place broken: their faces sat and broke each other. As suns, Sons gone tired in the heart and left the south. The North, years later she'd wept for him drunk and a man finally they must have thought. In the dark, he was even darker. Wooden fingers running. Wind so sweet it drank him.

Faces broke. Charts of age. Worn thru, to see black years. Bones in iron faces. Steel bones. Cages of decay. Cobblestones are wet near the army stores. Beer smells, Saturday. To now, they have passed so few lovely things.

Newsreel chickens. Browned in the street. I was carrying groceries back across the manicured past. Back, in a coat. Sunk, screaming at my fingers. Faces broken, hair waved, simple false elegance. I must tell someone I love you. Them. In line near the fence. She sucked my tongue. Red, actual red, but colored hair. Soft thin voice, and red freckles. A servant.

You should be ashamed. Your fingers are trembling. You lied in the garage. You lied yesterday. Get out of

the dance, down the back stairs, the street, and across
in the car. Run past it, around the high building. Court
Street, past the Y, harder, buttoning a cardigan, to Mor-
ton Street. Duck down, behind the car. Let Apple pass;
a few others. Now take off back down Court, the small
guys couldn't run. Cross High, near Graychun's, the
Alumni House, donald the fag's, the jews, to Kinney. Up
one block, crooked old jews die softly under the moon.
Past them. Past them. Their tombs and bones. Wet dollars blown against the fence. Past them, mattie's Dr.,
waltine, turn at Quitman. You can slow some, but not
too much. Through the Owl Club, Frankie, Dee's dumb
brother, turn, wave at them. Down the back steps, to
dirt, then stone. The poolroom, eddie smiles, points
at his hat, pats his car keys, phone numbers. Somerset
and the projects. To Montgomery and twist at Barclay.
Light people stare. Parties, relationships forming to be
explained later. Casual strangers' faces known better
than any now. Wood jaws sit open, their halls reek,
his fingers tug at yellow cotton pants and slip inside.
One finger her eyes open and close—her mouth opens
moaning deep agitated darkly.

In the middle of the street, straight at the moon.
Don't get close to the buildings. Too many exits, doors,
parks. Straight at the moon, up Barclay. Green tyrolean, gray bells, bucks. The smoking lights at Spruce. Hip

charles curtis. But turn before Herman or Wattley. They pace in wool jails, wool chains, years below the earth. Dead cocks crawling, eyes turned up in space. Near diane's house and the trees cradling her hidden flesh. Her fingers, her mouth, her eyes were all I had. And she screams now through soft wrinkles for me to take her. A Nun.

Wheeling now, back on the sidewalk, Saturday drunks spinning by, fish stores yawned, sprawled niggers dying without matches. Friends, enemies, strangers, fags, screaming louder than all sound. Young boys in hallways touching. Bulldaggers hiding their pussies. Black dead faces slowly ground to dust.

Headlight, Bubbles, Kennie, Rogie, Junie Boy, T. Bone, Rudy (All Hillside Place) or Sess, Ray, Lillian, Ungie, Ginger, Shirley, Cedie Abrams. Past them, displaced, blood seeps on the pavement under marquees. Lynn Hope marches on Belmont Ave. with us all. The Three Musketeers at the National. (Waverly Projects.) Past that. Their arms waving from the stands. Sun and gravel or the 3 hole opens and it's more beautiful than Satie. A hip, change speeds, head fake, stop, cut back, a hip, head fake . . . then only one man coming from the side . . . it went thru my head a million times, the years it took, seeing him there, with a good angle, shooting in, with 3 yards to the sidelines, about 10 home. I watched him all my life close in, and thot to cut, stop or bear down and pray I had speed. Answers shot up, but my head was full of blood and it moved me without talk. I stopped still the ball held almost like a basketball, wheeled and moved in to score untouched.

*   *   *

A long stretch from Waverly to Spruce (going the other way near Hillside). A long stretch, and steeper, straight up Spruce. And that street moved downtown. They all passed by, going down. And I was burning by, up the hill, toward The Foxes and the milk bar. Change clothes on the street to a black suit. Black wool.

4 corners, the entire world visible from there. Even to the lower regions.

The Alternative

This may not seem like much, but it makes a difference. And then there are those who prefer to look their fate in the eyes.

Between Yes and No
—Camus

The leader sits straddling the bed, and the night, tho innocent, blinds him. (Who is our flesh. Our lover, marched here from where we sit now sweating and remembering. Old man. Old man, find me, who am your only blood.)

Sits straddling the bed under a heavy velvet canopy. Homemade. The door opened for a breeze, which will not come through the other heavy velvet hung at the opening. (Each thread a face, or smell, rubbed against himself with yellow glasses and fear at their exposure. Death. Death. They (the younger students) run by screaming. Tho impromptu. Tho dead, themselves.

The leader, at his bed, stuck with 130 lbs. black meat sewed to failing bone. A head with big red eyes turning senselessly. Five toes on each foot. Each foot needing washing. And hands that dangle to the floor, tho the boy himself is thin small washed out, he needs huge bleak hands that drag the floor. And a head full of walls and flowers. Blinking lights. He is speaking.

"Yeh?" The walls are empty, heat at the ceiling. Tho one wall is painted with a lady. (Her name now. In large relief, a faked rag stuck between the chalk marks of her sex. Finley. Teddy's Doris. There sprawled where the wind fiddled with the drying cloth. Leon came in and laughed. Carl came in and hid his mouth, but he laughed. Teddy said, "Aw, Man."

"Come on, Hollywood. You can't beat that. Not with your years. Man, you're a schoolteacher 10 years after weeping for this old stinking bitch. And hit with a aspirin bottle (myth says)."

The leader is sprawled, dying. His retinue walks into their comfortable cells. "I have duraw-ings," says Leon, whimpering now in the buses from Chicago. Dead in a bottle. Floats out of sight, until the Africans arrive with love and prestige. "Niggers." They say. "Niggers." Be happy your ancestors are recognized in this burg. Martyrs. Dead in an automat, because the boys had left. Lost in New York, frightened of the burned lady, they fled into those streets and sang their homage to the Radio City.

The leader sits watching the window.

The dried orange glass etched with the fading wind. (How many there then? 13 rue Madeleine. The Boys Club. They give, what he has given them. Names. And the black cloth hung on the door swings back and forth. One pork chop on the hot plate. And how many there. Here, now. Just the shadow, waving its arms. The eyes tearing or staring blindly at the dead street. These same who loved me all my life. These same I find my senses in. Their flesh a wagon of dust, a mind conceived from all minds. A country, of thought. Where I am, will go, have never left. A love, of love. And the silence the question posed each second. "Is this my mind, my feeling. Is this voice something heavy in the locked streets of the universe. Dead ends. Where their talk (these nouns) is bitter vegetable." That is, the suitable question rings against the walls. Higher learning. That is, the moon through the window clearly visible. The leader in seersucker, reading his books. An astronomer of sorts. "Will you look at that? I mean, really, now, fellows. Cats!" (Which was Smitty from the City's entree. And him the smoothest of you American types. Said, "Cats. Cats. What's goin' on?" The debate.

The leader's job (he keeps it still, above the streets, summers of low smoke, early evening drunk and wobbling thru the world. He keeps it, baby. You dig?) was absolute. "I have the abstract position of watching these halls. Walking up the stairs giggling. Hurt under the cement steps, weeping . . . is my only task. Tho I play hockey with the broom & wine bottles. And am the sole martyr of this cause. A.B., Young Rick, T.P., Carl, Hambrick, Li'l Cholley, Phil. O.K. All their knowledge "Flait! More! Way!" The leader's job . . . to make attention for the place. Sit along the sides of the water or lay quietly back under his own shooting vomit, happy to die in a new gray suit. Yes. "And what not."

How many here now? Danny. (brilliant dirty curly Dan, the m.d.) Later, now, where you off to, my man. The tall skinny farmers, lucky to find sales and shiny white shoes. Now made it socially against the temples. This "hotspot" Darien drunk teacher blues . . . "and she tried to come on like she didn't even like to fuck. I mean, you know the kind . . ." The hand extended, palm upward. I place my own in yours. That cross, of feeling. Willie, in his grinning grave, has it all. The place, of all souls, in their greasy significance. An armor, like the smells drifting slowly up Georgia. The bridge players change clothes, and descend. Carrying home the rolls.

Jimmy Lassiter, first looie. A vector. What is the angle made if a straight line is drawn from the chapel, across to Jimmy, and connected there, to me, and back up the hill again? The angle of progress. "I was talkin' to ol' Mordecai yesterday in a dream, and it's me sayin' 'dig baby, why don't you come off it?' You know."

The
line, for Jimmy's sad and useless horn. And they tell
me (via phone, letter, accidental meetings in the Village. "Oh he's in med school and married and lost to
you, hombre." Ha. They don't dig completely where
I'm at. I have him now, complete. Though it is a vicious
sadness cripples my fingers. Those blue and empty
afternoons I saw him walking at my side. Criminals in
that world. Complete heroes of our time. (add Allen to
complete an early splinter group. Muslim heroes with
flapping pants. Raincoats. Trolley car romances.)

And
it's me making a portrait of them all. That was the leader's job. Alone with them. (Without them. Except beautiful faces shoved out the window, sunny days, I ran to
meet my darkest girl. Ol' Doll. "Man, that bitch got a
goddamn new car." And what not. And it's me sayin' to
her, Baby, knock me a kiss.

Tonight the leader is faced
with decision. Brown had found him drunk and weeping among the dirty clothes. Some guy with a crippled
arm had reported to the farmers (a boppin' gang gone
social. Sociologists, artistic arbiters of our times). This
one an athlete of mouselike proportions. "You know,"
he said, his withered arm hung stupidly in the rayon
suit, "that cat's nuts. He was sittin' up in that room

last night with dark glasses on . . . with a yellow bulb . . . pretendin' to read some abstract shit." (Damn, even the color wrong. Where are you now, hippy, under this abstract shit. Not even defense. That you remain forever in that world. No light. Under my fingers. That you exist alone, as I make you. Your sin, a final ugliness to you. For the leopards, all thumbs jerked toward the sand.) "Man, we do not need cats like that in the frat." (Agreed.)

Tom comes in with two big bottles of wine. For the contest. An outing. "Hugh Herbert and W.C. Fields will now indian wrestle for ownership of this here country!" (Agreed.) The leader loses . . . but is still the leader because he said some words no one had heard of before. (That was after the loss.)

Yng Rick has fucked someone else. Let's listen. "Oh, man, you cats don't know what's happenin'." (You're too much, Rick. Much too much. Like Larry Darnell in them ol' italian schools. Much too much.) "Babes" he called them (a poor project across from the convents. Baxter Terrace. Home of the enemy. We stood them off. We Cavaliers. And then, even tho Johnny Boy was his hero. Another midget placed on the purple. Early leader, like myself. The fight of gigantic proportions to settle all those ancient property disputes would have been between us. Both weighing close to 125. But I avoided that like the plague, and managed three times to drive past him with good hooks without incident. Whew, I said to Love, Whew. And Rick, had gone away from them, to school. Like myself. And now, strangely, for the Gods are white our teachers said, he found himself with me. And all the gold and diamonds of the crown I wore he hated. Though, the new wine settled, and his social graces kept him far enough away to ease the hurt of serving a hated master. Hence "babes," and the constant reference to his wiggling flesh. Listen.

"Yeh. Me and Chris had these D.C. babes at their cribs." (Does a dance step with the suggestive flair.) "Oooooo, that was some good box."

Tom knew immediately where that bit was at. And he pulled Rick into virtual madness . . . lies at least. "Yeh, Rick. Yeh? You mean you got a little Jones, huh? Was it good?" (Tom pulls on Rick's sleeve like Laurel and Rick swings.)

"Man, Tom, you don't have to believe it, baby. It's in here now!" (points to his stomach.)

The leader stirs. "Hmm, that's a funny way to fuck." Rick will give a boxing demonstration in a second.

Dick Smith smiles, "Wow, Rick you're way," extending his hand, palm upward. "And what not," Dick adds, for us to laugh. "O.K., you're bad." (At R's crooked jab.) "Huh, this cat always wants to bust somebody up, and what not. Hey, baby, you must be frustrated or something. How come you don't use up all that energy on your babes . . . and what not?"

The rest there, floating empty nouns. Under the sheets. The same death as the crippled fag. Lost with no defense. Except they sit now, for this portrait . . . in which they will be portrayed as losers. Only the leader wins. Tell him that.

Some guys playing cards. Some talking about culture, i.e., the leader had a new side. (Modesty denies. They sit around, in real light. The leader in his green glasses, fidgeting with his joint. Carl, in a brown fedora, trims his toes and nails. Spars with Rick. Smells his foot and smiles. Brady reads, in his silence, a crumpled black dispatch. Shorter's liver smells the hall and Leon slams the door, waiting for the single chop, the leader might have to share. The door opens, two farmers come in, sharp in orange suits. The hippies laugh, and hide their youthful lies. "Man, I was always hip. I mean, I knew about Brooks Brothers when I was 10." (So sad we never know the truth. About that world, until the bones dry in our heads. Young blond governors with their "dads" hip at the age of 2. That way. Which, now, I sit in judgment of. What I wanted those days with the covers of books turned toward the audience. The first nighters.

Or dragging my two forward to the Music Box to see Elliot Nugent. They would say, these dead men, laughing at us, "The natives are restless," stroking their gouty feet. Gimme culture, culture, culture, and Romeo and Juliet over the emerson.

How many there now? Make it 9. Phil's cracking the books. Jimmy Jones and Pud, two D.C. boys, famous and funny, study "zo" at the top of their voices. "Hemiptera," says Pud. "Homoptera," says Jimmy. "Weak as a bitch," says Phil, "both your knowledges are flait."

More than 9. Mazique, Enty, operating now in silence. Right hands flashing down the cards. "Uhh!" In love with someone, and money from home. Both perfect, with curly hair. "Uhh! Shit, Enty, hearts is trumps."

"What? Ohh, shit!"

"Uhh!", their beautiful hands flashing under the single bulb.

Hambrick comes with liquor. (A box of fifths, purchased with the fantastic wealth of his father's six shrimp shops.) "You cats caint have all this goddam booze. Brown and I got dates, that's why and we need some for the babes."

Brown has hot dogs for five. Franks, he says. "Damn, Cholley, you only get a half of frank . . . and you take the whole motherfucking thing."

"Aww, man, I'll pay you back." And the room, each inch, is packed with lives. Make it 12 . . . all heroes, or dead. Indian chiefs, the ones not waging their wars, like Clark, in the legal mist of Baltimore. A judge. Old Clark. You remember when we got drunk together and you fell down the stairs? Or that time you fell in the punch bowl puking, and let that sweet yellow ass get away? Boy, I'll never forget that, as long as I live. (Having died seconds later, he talks thru his rot.) Yeh, boy, you were always a card. (White man talk. A card. Who the hell says that, except that branch office with no culture. Piles of bullion, and casual violence. To the mind. Nights they kick you against the buildings. Communist homosexual nigger. "Aw, man, I'm married and got two kids."

What could be happening? Some uproar. "FUCK YOU, YOU FUNNY LOOKING SUNAFABITCH."

"Me? Funnylooking? Oh, wow. Will you listen to this little pointy head bastard calling *me* funny looking. Hey, Everett. Hey Everett! Who's the funniest looking . . . me or Keyes?"

"Aww, both you cats need some work. Man, I'm trying to read."

"Read? What? You gettin' into them books, huh? Barnes is whippin' your ass, huh? I told you not to take Organic . . . as light as you are."

"Shit. I'm not even thinking about Barnes. Barnes can kiss my ass."

"Shit. You better start thinking about him, or you'll punch right out. They don't need lightweights down in the valley. Ask Ugly Wilson."

"Look, Tom, I wasn't bothering you."

"Bothering me? Wha's the matter with you ol' Jimmy. Commere boy, lemme rub your head."

"Man, you better get the hell outta here."

"What? . . . Why? What you gonna do? You can't fight, you little funny looking buzzard."

"Hey, Tom, why you always bothering ol' Jimmy Wilson. He's a good man."

"Oh, oh, here's that little light ass Dan sticking up for Ugly again. Why you like him, huh? Cause he's the only cat uglier than you? Huh?"

"Tom's the worst looking cat on campus calling me ugly."

"Well, you are. Wait, lemme bring you this mirror so you can see yourself. Now, what you think. You can't think anything else."

"Aww, man, blow, will you?"

The pork chop is cooked and little charlie is trying to cut a piece off before the leader can stop him. "Ow, goddam."

"Well, who told you to try to steal it, jive ass."

"Hey, man, I gotta get somea that chop."

"Gimme some, Ray."

"Why don't you cats go buy something to eat. I didn't ask anybody for any of those hot dogs. So get away from my grease. Hungry ass spooks."

"Wait a minute, fella. I know you don't mean Young Rick."

"Go ask one of those D.C. babes for something to eat. I know they must have something you could sink your teeth into."

Pud and Jimmy Jones are wrestling under Phil's desk.

A.B. is playin' the dozen with Leon and Teddy. "Teddy are your momma's legs as crooked as yours?"

"This cat always wants to talk about people's mothers! Country bastard."

Tom is pinching Jimmy Wilson. Dan is laughing at them.

Enty and Mazique are playing bridge with the farmers. "Uhh! Beat that, jew boy!"

"What the fuck is trumps?"

The leader is defending his pork chop from Cholley, Rick, Brady, Brown, Hambrick, Carl, Dick Smith, (S from the City has gone out catting.

"Who is it?"

A muffled voice, under the uproar, "It's Mister Bush."

"Bush? Hey, Ray . . . Ray."

"Who is it?"

Plainer. "Mister Bush." (Each syllable pronounced and correct as a soft southern american can.) Innocent VIII in his bedroom shoes. Gregory at Canossa, raging softly in his dignity and power. "Mister Bush."

"Ohh, shit. Get that liquor somewhere. O.K., Mr. Bush, just a second . . . Not there, asshole, in the drawer."

"Mr. McGhee, will you kindly open the door."

"Ohh, shit, the hot plate. I got it." The leader turns a wastepaper basket upside-down on top of the chop. Swings open the door. "Oh, hello Mister Bush. How are you this evening?" About 15 boots sit smiling toward the door. Come in, Boniface. What news of Luther? In unison, now.

"Hi . . . Hello . . . How are you, Mister Bush?"

"Uh, huh."

He stares around the room, grinding his eyes into their various hearts. An unhealthy atmosphere, this America. "Mr. McGhee, why is it if there's noise in this dormitory it always comes from this room?" Aww, he knows. He wrote me years later in the air force that he knew, even then.

"What are you running here, a boys' club?" (That's it.) He could narrow his eyes even in that affluence. Put his hands on his hips. Shove that stomach at you as proof he was an authority of the social grace . . . a western man, no matter the color of his skin. How To? He was saying, this is not the way. Don't act like that word. Don't fail us. We've waited for all you handsome boys too long. Erect a new world, of lies and stocking caps. Silence, and a reluctance of memory. Forget the slow grasses, and flame, flame in the valley. Feet bound, dumb eyes begging for darkness. The bodies moved with the secret movement of the air. Swinging. My beautiful grandmother kneels in the shadow weeping. Flame, flame in the valley. Where is it there is light? Where, this music rakes my talk?

"Why is it, Mr. McGhee, when there's some disturbance in this building, it always comes from here?" (Aww, you said that . . .)

"And what are all you other gentlemen doing in here? Good night, there must be twenty of you here! Really, gentlemen, don't any of you have anything to do?" He made to smile, Ha, I know some of you who'd better be in your rooms right now hitting those books . . . or you might not be with us next semester. Ha.

"O.K., who is that under that sheet?" (It was Enty, a student dormitory director, hiding under the sheets, flat on the leader's bed.) "You, sir, whoever you are, come out of there, hiding won't do you any good. Come out!" (We watched the sheet, and it quivered. Innocent raised his finger.) "Come out, sir!" (The sheet pushed

slowly back. Enty's head appeared. And Bush more embarrassed than he.) "Mr. Enty! My assistant dormitory
director, good night. A man of responsibility. Go-od
night! Are there any more hiding in here, Mr. McGhee?"

"Not that I know of."

"Alright, Mr. Enty, you come with me. And the rest
of you had better go to your rooms and try to make some
better grades. Mr. McGhee, I'll talk to you tomorrow
morning in my office."

The leader smiles, "Yes." (Jive
ass.)

Bush turns to go, Enty following sadly. "My God,
what's that terrible odor . . . something burning." (The
leader's chop, and the wastepaper, under the basket,
starting to smoke.) "Mr. McGhee, what's that smell?"

"Uhhh." (come-on, baby) "Oh, it's Strothers' kneepads on the radiator! (Yass) They're drying."

"Well, Jesus,
I hope they dry soon. Whew! And don't forget, tomorrow morning, Mr. McGhee and you other gentlemen
had better retire, it's 2 in the morning!" The door slams.
Charlie sits where Enty was. The bottles come out. The
basket is turned right-side up. Chop and most of the
papers smoking. The leader pours water onto the mess
and sinks to his bed.

"Damn. Now I have to go hungry. Shit."

"That was pretty slick, ugly, the kneepads! Why

don't you eat them they look pretty done."

The talk is to that. That elegance of performance. The rite of lust, or self-extinction. Preservation. Some leave, and a softer uproar descends. Jimmy Jones and Pud wrestle quietly on the bed. Phil quotes the *Post*'s sport section on Willie Mays. Hambrick and Brown go for franks. Charlie scrapes the "burn" off the chop and eats it alone. Tom, Dan, Ted and the leader drink and manufacture lives for each person they know. We know. Even you. Tom, the lawyer. Dan, the lawyer. Ted, the high-school teacher. All their proper ways. And the leader, without cause or place. Except talk, feeling, guilt. Again, only those areas of the world make sense. Talk. We are doing that now. Feeling: that too. Guilt. That inch of wisdom, forever. Except he sits reading in green glasses. As, "No, no, the utmost share/Of my desire shall be/Only to kiss that air/That lately kissèd thee."

"Uhh! What's trumps, dammit!"

As, "Tell me not, Sweet, I am unkind,/That from the nunnery/Of thy chaste breast and quiet mind/To war and arms I fly."

"You talking about a lightweight mammy-tapper, boy, you really king."

Oh, Lucasta, find me here on the bed, with hard pecker and dirty feet. Oh, I suffer, in my green glasses, under the canopy of my loves. Oh, I am drunk and vomity in my room, with only Charlie Ventura to understand my grace. As, "Hardly are those words out when a vast image out of *Spiritus Mundi*/ Troubles my sight: somewhere in sands of the desert/A shape with lion body and the head of a man/A gaze blank and pitiless as the sun,/Is moving its slow thighs, while all about it/Reel shadows of the indignant desert birds."

Primers for dogs who are learning to read. Tinkle of European teacups. All longing, speed, suffering. All adventure, sadness, stink and wisdom. All feeling, silence, light. As, "Crush, O sea the cities with their catacomb-like corridors/And crush eternally the vile people,/The idiots, and the abstemious, and mow down, mow down/With a single stroke the bent backs of the shrunken harvest!"

"Damn, Charlie, we brought back a frank for everybody . . . now you want two. Wrong sunafabitch!"

"Verde que te quiero verde./Verde viento. Verdes ramas./El barco sobre la mar/y el caballo en la montaña."

"Hey, man, I saw that ol' fagit Bobby Hutchens down in the lobby with a real D.C. queer. I mean a real way-type sissy."

"Huh, man, he's just another *actor* . . . hooo."

"That cat still wearing them funny lookin' pants?"

"Yeh, and orange glasses. Plus, the cat always needs a haircut, and what not."

"Hey, man, you cats better cool it . . . you talkin' about Ray's main man. You dig?"

"Yeh. I see this cat easin' around corners with the cat all the time. I mean, talkin' some off-the-wall shit, too, baby."

"Yeh. Yeh. Why don't you cats go fuck yourselves or something hip like that, huh?"

"O.K., ugly Tom, you better quit inferring that shit about Ray. What you trying to say, ol' pointy head is funny or something?"

"*Funny . . . how the sound of your voice . . . thri-ills me. Strange . . .*" (the last à la King Cole.)

"Fuck you cats and your funny looking families too."

A wall. With light at the top, perhaps. No, there is light. Seen from both sides, a gesture of life. But always more than is given. An abstract infinitive. To love. To lie. To want. And that always . . . to want. Always, more than is given. The dead scramble up each side . . . words or drunkenness. Praise, to the flesh. Rousseau, Hobbes, and their betters. All move, from flesh to love. From love to flesh. At that point under the static light. It could be Shostakovich in Charleston, South Carolina. Or in the dull windows of Chicago, an unread volume of Joyce. Some black woman who will never hear the word *Negress* or remember your name. Or a thin preacher who thinks your name is Stephen. A wall. Oh, Lucasta.

"Man,

you cats don't know anything about Hutchens. I don't see why you talk about the cat and don't know the first thing about him."

"Shit. If he ain't funny . . . Skippy's a punk."

"How come you don't say that to Skippy?"

"Our Own Boy, Skippy Weatherson. All-coon fullback for 12 years."

"You tell him that!"

"Man, don't try to change the subject. This cat's trying to keep us from talking about his boy, Hutchens."

"Yeh, mammy-rammer. What's happenin' McGhee, ol' man?"

"Hooo. Yeh. They call this cat Dick Brown. Hoooo!"

Rick moves to the offensive. The leader in his book, or laughs, "Aww, man, that cat ain't my boy. I just don't think you cats ought to talk about people you don't know anything about! Plus, that cat probably gets more ass than any of you silly-ass mother fuckers."

"Hee. That Ray sure can pronounce that word. I mean he don't say mutha like most folks . . . he always pronounces the mother *and* the fucker, so proper. And it sure makes it sound nasty." (A texas millionaire talking.)

"Hutchens teachin' the cat how to talk . . . that's what's happening. Ha. In exchange for services rendered!"

"Wait, Tom. Is it you saying that Hutchens and my man here are into some funny shit?"

"No, man. It's you saying that. It was me just inferring, you dig?"

"Hey, why don't you cats just get drunk in silence, huh?"

"Hey, Bricks, what was Hutchens doin' downstairs with that cat?"

"Well, they were just coming in the dormitory, I guess. Hutchens was signing in that's all."

"Hey, you dig . . . I bet he's takin' that cat up to his crib."

"Yeh, I wonder what they into by now. Huh! Probably suckin' the shit out of each other."

"Aww, man, cool it, willya . . . Damn!"

"What's the matter, Ray, you don't dig love?"

"Hey, it's Young Rick saying that we oughta go up and dig what's happenin' up there?"

"Square mother fucker!"

"Votre mere!"

"Votre mere noir!"

"Boy, these cats in French One think they hip!"

"Yeh, let's go up and see what those cats are doing."

"Tecch, aww, shit. Damn, you some square cats, wow! Cats got nothing better to do than fuck with people. Damn!"

Wall. Even to move, impossible. I sit, now, forever where I am. No further. No farther. Father, who am I to hide myself? And brew a world of soft lies.

Again. "Verde
que te quiero verde." Green. Read it again, Il Duce. Make
it build some light here . . . where there is only darkness. Tell them "Verde, que te quiero verde." I want you
Green. Leader, the paratroopers will come for you at
noon. A helicopter low over the monastery. To get you
out.

But my country. My people. These dead souls, I call
my people. Flesh of my flesh.

At noon, Il Duce. Make
them all etceteras. Extras. The soft strings behind the
final horns.

"Hey, Ray, you comin' with us?"

"Fuck you cats. I got other things to do."

"Damn, now the cat's trying to pretend he can read
Spanish."

"Yeh . . . well let's go see what's happening cats."

"Cats, Cats, Cats . . . What's happenin'?"

"Hey, Smitty! We going upstairs to peep that ol'
sissy Hutchens. He's got some big time D.C. faggot in
there with him. You know, we figured it'd be better
than 3-D."

"Yeh? That's pretty hip. You not coming, Ray?"

"No, man . . . I'm sure you cats can peep in a key-
hole without me."

"Bobby's his main man, that's all."

"Yeh, mine and your daddy's."

Noise. Shouts, and Rick begs them to be softer. For the circus. Up the creaking stairs, except Carl and Leon who go to the freshman dorm to play ping-pong . . . and Ted who is behind in his math.

The 3rd floor of Park Hall, an old 19th-century philanthropy, gone to seed. The missionaries' words dead & hung useless in the air. "Be clean, thrifty, and responsible. Show the anti-Christs you're ready for freedom and God's true word." Peasants among the mulattoes, and the postman's son squats in his glasses shivering at his crimes.

"Hey, which room is his?"

"Three Oh Five."

"Hey, Tom, how you know the cat's room so good? This cat must be sneaking too."

"Huhh, yeh!"

"O.K. Rick, just keep walking."

"Here it is."

"Be cool, bastard. Shut up."

They stood and grinned. And punched each other. Two bulbs in the hall. A window at each end. One facing the reservoir, the other, the fine-arts building where Professor Gorsun sits angry at jazz. "Goddamnit, none of that nigger music in my new building. Culture. Goddamnit, ladies and gentlemen, line up and be baptized. This pose will take the hurt away. We are white and featureless under this roof. Praise God, from whom all blessings flow!"

"Bobby. Bobby, baby."

"Huh?"

"Don't go blank on me like that, baby. I was saying something."

"Oh, I'm sorry . . . I guess I'm just tired or something."

"I was saying, how can you live in a place like this. I mean, really, baby, this place is nowhere. Whew. It's like a jail or something eviler."

"Yes, I know."

"Well, why don't you leave it then. You're much too sensitive for a place like this. I don't see why you stay in this damn school. You know, you're really talented."

"Yeh, well, I figured I have to get a degree, you know. Teach or something, I suppose. There's not really much work around for spliv actors."

"Oh, Bobby, you ought to stop being so conscious of being colored. It really is not fashionable. Ummm. You know you have beautiful eyes."

"You want another drink, Lyle?"

"Ugg. Oh, that

cheap bourbon. You know I have some beautiful wines at home. You should try drinking some good stuff for a change. Damn, Bob, why don't you just leave this dump and move into my place? There's certainly enough room. And we certainly get along. Ummm. Such beautiful eyes and hair too."

"Hah. How much rent would I have to pay out there? I don't have penny the first!"

"Rent? No, no . . . you don't have to worry about that. I'll take care of all that. I've got one of those gooood jobs, honey. US guvment."

"Oh? Where do you work?"

"The P.O. with the rest of the fellas. But it's enough for what I want to do. And you wouldn't be an expense. Hmmp. Or would you? You know you have the kind of strong masculine hands I love. Like you could crush anything you wanted. Lucky I'm on your good side. Hmmp."

"Well, maybe at the end of this semester I could leave. If the offer still holds then."

"Still holds? Well why not? We'll still be friends then, I'm certain. Ummm. Say, why don't we shut off that light."

"Umm. Let me do it. There . . . You know I loved you in Jimmy's play, but the rest of those people are really just kids. You were the only person who really understood what was going on. You have a strong maturity that comes through right away. How old are you, Bobby?"

"Nineteen."

"O baby . . . that's why your skin is so soft. Yes. Say, why wait until the end of the semester . . . that's two months away. I might be dead before that, you know. Umm."

The wind moves thru the leader's room, and he sits alone, under the drooping velvet, repeating words he does not understand. The yellow light burns. He turns it off. Smokes. Masturbates. Turns it on. Verde, verde. Te quiero. Smokes. And then to his other source. "Yma's brother," Tom said when he saw it. "Yma Sumac, Albert Camus. Man, nobody wants to go by their right names no more. And a cat told me that chick ain't really from Peru. She was born in Brooklyn, man, and her name's Camus too. Amy Camus. This cat's name is probably Trebla Sumac, and he ain't French he's from Brooklyn too. Yeh. Ha!"

In the dark the words are anything. "If it is true that the only paradise is that which one has lost, I know what name to give that something tender and inhuman which dwells within me today."

"Oh, shit, fuck it. Fuck it." He slams the book against the wall, and empties Hambrick's bottle. "I mean, why?" Empties bottle. "Shiiit."

When he swings the door open the hall above is screams. Screams. All their voices, even now right here. The yellow glasses falling on the stairs, and broken. In his bare feet. "Shiit. Dumb ass cats!"

"Rick, Rick, what's the cat doing now?"

"Man, be cool. Ha, the cat's kissin' Hutchens on the face, man. Um-uhmm. Yeh, baby. Damn, he's puttin' his hands all over the cat. Aww, rotten motherfuckers!"

"What's happening?"

"Bastards shut out the lights!"

"Damn."

"Gaw-uhd damn!"

"Hey, let's break open the door."

"Yeh, HEY, YOU CATS, WHAT'S HAPPENING IN THERE, HUH?"

"Yeh. Hee, hee. OPEN UP, FAGGOTS!"

"Wheee! HEY LET US IN, GIRLS!"

Ricky and Jimmy run against the door, the others screaming and jumping, doors opening all along the hall. They all come out, screaming as well. "LET US IN. HEY, WHAT'S HAPPENIN', BABY!" Rick and Jimmy run against the door, and the door is breaking.

"Who is it? What do you want?" Bobby turns the light on, and his friend, a balding queer of 40, is hugged against the sink.

"Who are they, Bobby? What do they want?"

"Bastards. Damn if I know. GET OUTTA HERE, AND MIND YOUR OWN DAMN BUSINESS, YOU CREEPS. Creeps. Damn. Put on your clothes, Lyle!"

"God, they're trying to break the door down, Bobby. What they want? Why are they screaming like that?"

"GET THE HELL AWAY FROM THIS DOOR, GODDAMNIT!"

"YEH, YEH. WE SAW WHAT YOU WAS DOIN', HUTCHENS. OPEN THE DOOR AND LET US GET IN ON IT."

"WHEEEEEE! HIT THE FUCKING DOOR, RICK! HIT IT!"

And at the top of the stairs the leader stops, the whole hall full of citizens. Doctors, judges, first negro directors of welfare chain, morticians, chemists, ad men, fighters for civil rights, all admirable, useful men. "BREAK THE FUCKIN' DOOR OPEN, RICK! YEH!"

A wall. Against it, from where you stand, the sea stretches smooth for miles out. Their voices distant thuds of meat against the sand. Murmurs of insects. Hideous singers against your pillow every night of your life. They are there now, screaming at you.

"Ray, Ray, comeon man help us break this faggot's door!"

"Yeh, Ray, comeon!"

"Man, you cats are fools. Evil stupid fools!"

"What? Man, will you listen to this cat."

"Listen, hell, let's get this door. One more smash and it's in. Comeon, Brady, lets break the fuckin' thing."

"Yeh, comeon you cats, don't stand there listenin' to that pointy head clown, he just don't want us to pop his ol' lady!"

"YEH, YEH. LET'S GET IN THERE. HIT IT HIT IT!"

"Goddamnit. Goddamnit, get the fuck out of here. Get outta here. Damnit Rick, you sunafabitch, get the hell outtahere. Leave the cat alone!"

"Man, don't push me like that, you lil' skinny ass. I'll bust your jaw for you."

"Yeh? Yeh? Yeh? Well you come on, you lyin' ass. This cat's always talking about all his 'babes' and all he's got to do is sneak around peeping in keyholes. You big lying asshole . . . all you know how to do is bullshit and jerk off!"

"Fuck you, Ray."

"Your ugly ass mama."

"Shiit. You wanna go round with me, baby?"

"Comeon. Comeon, big time cocksman, comeon!"

Rick hits the leader full in the face, and he falls backward across the hall. The crowd follows screaming at this new feature.

"Aww, man, somebody stop this shit. Rick'll kill Ray!"

"Well, you stop it, man."

"O.K., O.K., cut it out. Cut it out, Rick. You win, man. Leave the cat alone. Leave him alone."

"Bad Rick . . . Bad Rick, Bad ass Rick!"

"Well, man, you saw the cat fuckin' with me. He started the shit!"

"Yeh . . . tough cat!"

"Get up, Ray."

And then the door does open and Bobby Hutchens stands in the half light in his shower shoes, a broom in his hands. The boys scream and turn their attention back to Love. Bald Lyle is in the closet. More noise. More lies. More prints in the sand, away, or toward some name. I am a poet. I am a rich famous butcher. I am the man who paints the gold balls on the tops of flagpoles. I am, no matter, more beautiful than anyone else. And I have come a long way to say this. Here. In the long hall, shadows across my hands. My face pushed hard against the floor. And the wood, old and protestant. And their voices, all these other selves screaming for blood. For blood, or whatever it is fills their noble lives.

The Largest Ocean
in the World

for Larry Wallrich

Toppled. Cold dark stone, spread thru the darker night.
And night. Again he would come down. Come thru it
settling fast, without breathing, as disguised as the
day itself had become. Sun dead. The bright instincts.
Hurdled, years before, after all had formed. Settled,
the ripples of weather, darkness, flesh, among the torn
stones.

He came down the stairs with motors crippling his
face. Where the brain sagged, and ran into deeper
colors. They spread. The walks ran together. Voices of
the students. Voices of the preachers. Voices of the simple past. Kept toward missions. All repose, response,
dulled. At last to a single dripping cock. It sat inside
his heart. And hardened at what the moon proposed.
What the night meant to have breathing around, and
so quiet, and so sure, and without the madness turned
him inside, killed him, made him, what you called "a
murderer."

The street was dark, without their hands. They slept. So, the street would not.

Whistling. He had his hands in the back pockets.

A thin man. A small boy. A naked thing for any who looked. For any would stick their mouths to his. Or watch him breathe. This man, boy, self, had not come here to see you. (Where you live now.) Had not asked you for your life, or proposed a vile connection, i.e., "I Love You": "Come With Me," or simpler, "Listen, Please, Listen To Me." But you had not lived then. Or come from where the things set up dark words in you.

This is an old song. Where the street, a wide avenue, turns and is lost as it approaches the river. Not knowing himself, or the town. Just what pushed him. He could move. He could move, himself. And scream, scream it to him. You, not some other, are like this. Were of this flesh. You, talk to him, pass him by, hold up a hand to see what he will say. Run, from you. (From me, who came back, now, in some fit, to play God.)

No one passed him on the street. Then someone did. Then a car went by. And one with a kissing couple slowed at a light, then pulled quickly toward the park. (Is it meaningful to speak of form, and say, there is a form love takes? As meaningful as the woman slumped in the hallway, weeping, under those coarse lights, weeping, for all her hurts, my own.)

How many worlds; for blood infests our minds. The

eye is its own creation. The fingers. There are men who live in themselves so they think their minds will create a different place of ecstasy. That it will love them.

A ridge of trees. Tall thin lights, lighting only the tops of leaves. Soft as it reached us. Harsh at the top, making shadows that moved without flesh.

A long sloping walk. His head had bent, was bent, always. (They will say that you are abstracted. That you are funny. That you are not what you seem, but evil. And fall out drunk and sick and shed that skin. Shed it now. To this. An "X" on the graph, where you paused.)

Up near the theaters, where the city changed. Was softer, grew wilder, and green even beneath the darkness. A drugstore at an intersection with the full white moon pressed under the glass. A tree at its edges, folding slowly. The dead fill the streets. And their dead thoughts. I do not know this place.

Seeing no one. Not wanting anyone. But you all. I want now to have all your minds. Want now, to be them. To feel all you feel. Think, your hundred thoughts. Sink down on your lover, and tell about myself. Yourself. (The thin boy at the corner, under the blurred lights, green tops and wires under the moon.) Seeing no one, and wanting, no one. Wanting. He could press himself against the darkness and suck it into himself. He could sit down here and weep. He could die. He could grow older, and find himself calmer, more detached, disposed to sit and talk with us about himself. He could find himself lying about his life, and see back across blood, to the blank marquee and quiet intersection of his discovery. Balboa. You have made your move. The waters move softly here. Blue clear warm water, barely moving. And smooth sand for miles. No one here. Or where you came from. (We will give a date for your madness, stretched at the sea's edge screaming at the new sun as it came up. We will say, of you, that you were always "alone.")

To move again. Let it sink in. (Let the waters turn, the ocean, mount. Huge waves, strike down trees. So far down beneath where you sprawled and watched the light change the water's pigment.)

Bells thread the night. He is twisting his hips like a young girl, hands in his hair. He is walking quietly, with his lips pinched and cheeks drawn to kiss someone. (He kisses his own hands, and smells their palms.) He is putting his hands on his flanks to feel them jerk, as he sways gently through his night. He is a soft young girl, running his hands over his own body. The bells shake the darkness. The waves draw up over all the land. But there was no one else. The girl is pulled under, and as the waters die she drifts facedown and quiet. It was getting light. More cars moved up the streets, and he waved at one.

Uncle Tom's Cabin:
Alternate Ending

"6½" *was* the answer. But it seemed to irritate Miss Orbach. Maybe not the answer—the figure itself—but the fact it should be there, and in such loose possession.

"OH who is he to know such a thing? That's really improper to set up such liberations. And moreso."

What came into her head next she could hardly understand. A breath of cold. She did shudder, and her fingers clawed at the tiny watch she wore hidden in the lace of the blouse her grandmother had given her when she graduated teacher's college.

Ellen, Eileen, Evelyn . . . Orbach. She could be any of them. Her personality was one of theirs. As specific and as vague. The kindly menace of leading a life in whose balance evil was a constant intrigue but grew uglier and more remote as it grew stronger. She would have loved to do something really dirty. But nothing she had ever heard of was dirty enough. So she contented herself with good, i.e., purity, as a refuge from mediocrity. But being unconscious, or largely remote from her own sources, she would only admit to the possibility of grace. Not God. She would not be trapped into *wanting* even God.

So remorse took her easily. For any reason. A reflection in a shop window, of a man looking in vain for her ankles. (Which she covered with heavy colorless woolen.) A sudden gust of warm damp air around her legs or face. Long dull rains that turned her from her books. Or, as was the case this morning, some completely uncalled-for shaking of her silent doctrinaire routines.

"6½" had wrenched her unwillingly to exactly where she was. Teaching the 5th grade, in a grim industrial complex of northeastern America; about 1942. And how the social doth pain the anchorite.

Nothing made much sense in such a context. People moved around, and disliked each other for no reason. Also, and worse, they said they loved each other, and usually for less reason, Miss Orbach thought. Or would have if she did.

And in this class sat 30 dreary sons and daughters of such circumstance. Specifically, the thriving children of the thriving urban lower middle classes. Postmen's sons and factory-worker debutantes. Making a great run for America, now prosperity and the war had silenced for a time the intelligent cackle of tradition. Like a huge gray bubbling vat the country, in its apocalyptic version of history and the future, sought now, in its equally apocalyptic profile of itself as it had urged swiftly its own death since the Civil War. To promise. Promise. And that to be that all who had ever dared to live here would die when the people and interests who had been its rulers died. The intelligent poor now were being admitted. And with them a great many Negroes . . . who would die when the rest of the dream died not even understanding that they, like Ishmael, should have been the sole survivors. But now they were being tricked. "6½" the boy said. After the fidgeting and awkward silence. One little black boy raised his hand, and looking at the tip of Miss Orbach's nose said 6½. And then he smiled, very embarrassed and very sure of being wrong.

I would have said, "No, boy, shut up and sit down. You are wrong. You don't know anything. Get out of here and be very quick. Have you no idea what you're getting involved in? My God . . . you nigger, get out of here and save yourself, while there's time. Now beat it." But those people had already been convinced. Read Booker T. Washington one day, when there's time. What that led to. The 6½'s moved for power . . . and there seemed no other way.

So three elegant Negroes in light gray suits grin and throw me through the window. They are happy and I am sad. It is an ample test of an idea. And besides, "6½" is the right answer to the woman's question.

[The psychological and the social. The spiritual and the practical. Keep them together and you profit, maybe, someday, come out on top. Separate them, and you go along the road to the commonest of Hells. The one we westerners love to try to make art out of.]

The woman looked at the little brown boy. He blinked at her, trying again not to smile. She tightened her eyes, but her lips flew open. She tightened her lips, and her eyes blinked like the boy's. She said, "How do you get that answer?" The boy told her. "Well, it's right," she said, and the boy fell limp, straining even harder to look sorry. The Negro in back of the answerer pinched him, and the boy shuddered. A little white girl next to him touched his hand, and he tried to pull his own hand away with his brain.

"Well, that's right, class. That's exactly right. You may sit down now, Mr. McGhee."

Later on in the day, after it had started exaggeratedly to rain very hard and very stupidly against the windows and soul of her 5th-grade class, Miss Orbach became convinced that the little boy's eyes were too large. And in fact they did bulge almost grotesquely white and huge against his bony heavy-veined skull. Also, his head was much too large for the rest of the scrawny body. And he talked too much, and caused too many disturbances. He also stared out the window when Miss Orbach herself would drift off into her sanctuary of light and hygiene even though her voice carried the inanities of arithmetic seemingly without delay. When she came back to the petty social demands of 20th-century humanism the boy would be watching something walk across the playground. OH, it just would not work.

She wrote a note to Miss Janone, the school nurse, and gave it to the boy, McGhee, to take to her. The note read: "Are the large eyes a sign of_____?"

Little McGhee, of course, could read, and read the note. But he didn't of course understand the last large word which was misspelled anyway. But he tried to memorize the note, repeating to himself over and over again its contents . . . sounding the last long word out in his head, as best he could.

Miss Janone wiped her big nose and sat the boy down, reading the note. She looked at him when she finished, then read the note again, crumpling it on her desk.

She looked in her medical book and found out what Miss Orbach meant. Then she said to the little Negro, Dr. Robard will be here in 5 minutes. He'll look at you. Then she began doing something to her eyes and fingernails.

When the doctor arrived he looked closely at McGhee and said to Miss Janone, "Miss Orbach is confused."

McGhee's mother thought that too. Though by the time little McGhee had gotten home he had forgotten the "long word" at the end of the note.

"Is Miss Orbach the woman who told you to say sangwich instead of sammich?" Louise McGhee giggled.

"No, that was Miss Columbe."

"Sangwich, my christ. That's worse than sammich. Though you better not let me hear you saying sammich either . . . like those Davises."

"I don't say sammich, mamma."

"What's the word then?"

"Sandwich."

"That's right. And don't let anyone tell you anything else. Teacher or otherwise. Now I wonder what that word could've been?"

"I donno. It was very long. I forgot it."

Eddie McGhee Sr. didn't have much of an idea what the word could be either. But he had never been to college like his wife. It was one of the most conspicuously dealt with factors of their marriage.

So the next morning Louise McGhee, after calling her office, the Child Welfare Bureau, and telling them she would be a little late, took a trip to the school, which was on the same block as the house where the McGhees lived, to speak to Miss Orbach about the long word which she suspected might be injurious to her son and maybe to Negroes In General. This suspicion had been bolstered a great deal by what Eddie Jr. had told her about Miss Orbach, and also equally by what Eddie Sr. had long maintained about the nature of White

People In General. "Oh well," Louise McGhee sighed, "I guess I better straighten this sister out." And that is exactly what she intended.

When the two McGhees reached the Center Street school the next morning Mrs. McGhee took Eddie along with her to the principal's office, where she would request that she be allowed to see Eddie's teacher.

Miss Day, the old lady principal, would then send Eddie to his class with a note for his teacher, and talk to Louise McGhee, while she was waiting, on general problems of the neighborhood. Miss Day was a very old woman who had despised Calvin Coolidge. She was also, in one sense, exotically liberal. One time she had forbidden old man Seidman to wear his pince-nez anymore, as they looked too snooty. Center Street sold more war stamps than any other grammar school in the area, and had a fairly good track team.

Miss Orbach was going to say something about Eddie McGhee's being late, but he immediately produced Miss Day's note. Then Miss Orbach looked at Eddie again, as she had when she had written her own note the day before.

She made Mary Ann Fantano the monitor and stalked off down the dim halls. The class had a merry time of it when she left, and Eddie won an extra 2 Nabisco graham crackers by kissing Mary Ann while she sat at Miss Orbach's desk.

When Miss Orbach got to the principal's office and pushed open the door she looked directly into Louise McGhee's large brown eyes, and fell deeply and hopelessly in love.

The Death of Horatio Alger

The cold red building burned my eyes. The bricks hung together, like the city, the nation, under the dubious cement of rationalism and need. A need so controlled, it only erupted out of the used-car lots, or sat parked, Saturdays, in front of our orange house, for Orlando, or Algernon, or Danny, or J.D. to polish. There was silence, or summers, noise. But this was a few days after Christmas, and the ice melted from the roofs and the almost frozen water knocked lethargically against windows, tar roofs and slow dogs moping through the yards. The building was Central Avenue School. And its tired red sat on the corner of Central Avenue and Dey (pronounced *die* by the natives, *day* by the teachers, or any nonresident whites) Street. Then, on Dey, halfway up the block, the playground took over. A tarred-over yard, though once there had been gravel, surrounded by cement and a wire metal fence.

The snow was dirty as it sat dull and melting near the Greek restaurants, and the dimly lit "grocey" stores of the Negroes. The rich boys had metal wagons the poor rode in. The poor made up games, the rich played them. The poor won the games, or as an emergency measure, the fights. No one thought of the snow except Mr. Feld, the playground director, who was in charge of it, or Miss Martin, the husky gym teacher Matthew Stodges had pushed into the cloakroom, who had no chains on her car. Gray slush ran over the curbs, and our dogs drank it out of boredom, shaking their heads and snorting.

I had said something about J.D.'s father, as to who he was, or had he ever been. And J., usually a confederate and private strong arm, broke bad because Augie, Norman, and white Johnny were there, and laughed, misunderstanding simple "dozens" with ugly insult, in that curious scholarship the white man affects when he suspects a stronger link than sociology, or the tired cultural lies of Harcourt, Brace sixth-grade histories. And under their naïveté he grabbed my shirt and pushed me in the snow. I got up, brushing dead ice from my ears, and he pushed me down again, this time dumping a couple pounds of cold dirty slush down my neck, calmly hysterical at his act.

J. moved away and stood on an icy garbage hamper, sullenly throwing wet snow at the trucks on Central Avenue. I pushed myself into a sitting position, shaking my head. Tears full in my eyes, and the cold slicing minutes from my life. I wasn't making a sound. I wasn't

thinking any thought I could make someone else understand. Just the rush of young fear and anger and disgust.
I could have murdered God, in that simple practical
way we kick dogs off the bottom step.

Augie (my best white friend), fat Norman, whose
hook shots usually hit the rim, and were good for easy
tip-ins by our big men, and useless white Johnny, who
had some weird disease that made him stare, even in
the middle of a game, he'd freeze, and sometimes line
drives almost knocked his head off while he shuddered
slightly, cracking and recracking his huge knuckles.
They were howling and hopping, they thought it was
so funny that J. and I had come to blows. And espe-
cially, I guess, that I had got my lumps. "Hey, wiseass,
somebody's gonna break your nose!" fat Norman would
say over and over whenever I did something to him.
Hold his pants when he tried his jump shot; spike him
sliding into home (he was a lousy catcher); talk about
his brother who hung out under the El and got naked
in alleyways.

* * *

(The clucks of Autumn could have, right at that moment, easily seduced me. Away, and into school. To
masquerade as a half-rich nigra with shiny feet. Back
through the clean station, and up the street. Stopping

to talk on the way. One beer gets you drunk and you stand in an empty corridor, lined with Italian paintings, talking about the glamours of sodomy.)

Rise and Slay.

I hurt so bad, and inside without bleeding I realized the filthy gray scratches my blood would carry to my heart. John walked off staring, and Augie and Norman disappeared, so easily there in the snow. And J.D. too, my first love, drifted against the easy sky. Weeping at what he'd done. No one there but me. THE SHORT SKINNY BOY WITH THE BUBBLE EYES.

Could leap up and slay them. Could hammer my fist and misery through their faces. Could strangle and bake them in the crude jungle of my feeling. Could stuff them in the sewie hole with the collected garbage of children's guilt. Could elevate them into heroic images of my own despair. A righteous messenger from the wrong side of the tracks. Gym teachers, cutthroats, aging pickets, ease by in the cold. The same lyric chart, exchange of particulars, that held me in my minutes, the time "Brownie" rammed the glass door down and ate up my suit. Even my mother, in a desperate fit of rhythm, was not equal to the task. Which was simple economics. I.e., a white man's dog cannot bite your son if he has been taught that something very ugly will happen to him if he does. He might pace stupidly in his ugly fur, but he will never never bite.

But what really stays to be found completely out, except stupid enterprises like art? The word on the page, the paint on the canvas (Marzette dragging in used-up canvases to revive their hopeless correspondence with the times), stone clinging to air, as if it were real. Or something a Deacon would admit was beautiful. The conscience rules against ideas. The point was to be where you wanted to, and do what you wanted to. After all is "said and done," what is left but those sheepish constructions. "I've got to go to the toilet" is no less pressing than the Puritans taking off for Massachusetts, and dragging their devils with them. (There is in those parts, even now, the peculiar smell of roasted sex organs. And when a good New Englander leaves his house in the earnestly moral sub-towns to go into the smoking hells of soon to be destroyed Yankee Gomorrahs, you watch him pull very firmly at his tie, or strapping on very tightly his evil watch.) The penitence there. The masochism. So complete and conscious a phenomenon. Like a standard of beauty; for instance, the bespectacled, soft-breasted, gently pigeon-toed maidens of America. Neither rich nor poor, with intelligent smiles and straight lovely noses. No one would think of them as beautiful but these mysterious scions of the Puritans. They value health and devotion, and their good women, the lefty power of all our nation, are unpresuming subtle beauties, who could even live with poets (if they are from the right stock), if pushed to that. But mostly they are where they should be, reading good books and opening windows to air out their bedrooms. And it is a useful memory here, because such things as these were the vague images that had even so early helped shape me. Light freckles, sandy hair, narrow clean bodies. Though none lived where I lived then. And I don't remember a direct look at them even, with clear knowledge of my desire, until one afternoon I gave a speech at East Orange High, as sports editor of our high school paper, which should have been printed in Italian, and I saw there, in the auditorium, young American girls, for the first time. And have loved them as flesh things emanating from real life, that is, in contrast to my own, a scraping and floating through the last three red and blue stripes of the flag, that settles the hash of the lower middle class. So that even sprawled there in the snow, with my blood and pompous isolation, I vaguely knew of a glamorous world and was mistaken into thinking it could be gotten from books. Negroes and Italians beat and shaped me, and my allegiance is there. But the triumph of romanticism was parquet floors, yellow dresses, gardens and sandy hair. I must have felt the loss and could not rise against a cardboard world of dark hair and linoleum. Reality was something I was convinced I could not have.

And thus to be flogged or put to the

rack. For all our secret energies. The first leap over the barrier: when the victim finds he can no longer stomach his own "group." Politics whinnies, but is still correct, and asleep in a windy barn. The beautiful statue of victory, whose arms were called duty. And they curdle in her snatch thrust there by angry minorities, along with their own consciences. Poets climb, briefly, off their motorcycles, to find out who owns their words. We are named by all the things we will never understand. Whether we can fight or not, or even at the moment of our hugest triumph we stare off into space remembering the snow melting in our cuts, and all the pimps of reason who've ever conquered us. It is the harshest form of love.

* * *

I could not see when I "chased" Norman and Augie. Chased in quotes because they really did not have to run. They could have turned, and myth aside, calmly whipped my ass. But they ran, laughing and keeping warm. And J.D. kicked snow from around a fire hydrant flatly into the gutter. Smiling and broken, with his head hung just slanted toward the yellow dog ice running down a hole. I took six or seven long running steps and tripped. I couldn't have been less interested, but the whole project had gotten out of hand. I was crying, and my hands were freezing, and the two white boys leaned against the pointed metal fence and laughed and slapped their knees. I threw snow stupidly in their direction. It fell short and was not even noticed as it dropped.

(All of it rings in your ears for a long time. But the payback . . . in simple terms against such actual sin as supposing quite confidently that the big sweating purple whore staring from her peed up hall very casually at your whipping has *never* been loved . . . is hard. We used to say.)

Then I pushed to my knees and could only see J. leaning there against the hydrant looking just over my head. I called to him, for help really. But the words rang full of dead venom. I screamed his mother a purple nigger with alligator titties. His father a bilious white man with sores on his jowls. I was screaming for help in my hatred and loss, and only the hatred would show. And he came over shouting for me to shut up. Shut up, skinny bastard. I'll break your ass if you don't. Norman had both hands on his stomach, his laugh was getting so violent, and he danced awkwardly toward us howling to agitate J. to beat me some more. But J. whirled on him perfectly and rapped him hard under his second chin. Norman was going to say, "Hey me-an," in that hated twist of our speech, and J. hit him again, between his shoulder and chest, and almost dropped him to his knees. Augie cooled his howl to a giggle of concern and backed up until Norman turned and they both went shouting up the street.

I got to my feet, wiping my freezing hands on my jacket. J. was looking at me hard, like country boys do, when their language, or the new tone they need to take on once they come to this cold climate (1940s New Jersey) fails, and they are left with only the old Southern tongue, which cruel farts like me used to deride their lack of interest in America. I turned to walk away. Both my eyes were nothing but water, though it held at their rims, stoically refusing to blink and thus begin to sob uncontrollably. And to keep from breaking down I wheeled and hid the weeping by screaming at that boy. You nigger without a father. You eat your mother's pussy. And he wheeled me around and started to hit me again.

Someone called my house and my mother and father and grandmother and sister were strung along Dey Street, in some odd order. (They couldn't have come out of the house "together.") And I was conscious first of my father saying, "Go on, Mickey, hit him. Fight back." And for a few seconds, under the weight of that plea for my dignity, I tried. I feinted and danced, but I couldn't even roll up my fists. The whole street was blurred and hot as my eyes. I swung and swung, but J.D. bashed me when he wanted to.

My mother stopped the fight finally, shuddering at the thing she'd made. "His hands are frozen, Michael. His hands are frozen." And my father looks at me even now, wondering if they'll ever thaw.

Going Down Slow

Ah, miserable, thou, to whom Truth, in her first tides, bears nothing
but wrecks

—Melville

In his mind Lew Crosby was already at Mauro's loft. But
the soft neon rain and long wet city streets caused the
separation. The logical affront of reason, or imagination,
staled into thinking of itself as reality, or "a reality." As
mediocre neo-freudians always say in bars, leaning on
one arm, half to themselves, "That's your reality."

But Crosby was no neo-freudian, so he measured a
real distance on top of his fantasy, and continued very
swiftly to walk. If he was a neo-anything, and this was
his own thinking, he was a neo-shithead, a neo-dope.
He opened his mouth pretending to talk to himself so
the curiously refreshing drizzle would spray onto his
tongue. He pretended talking to himself, like a Genet
heroine pretending he is a woman. The more fully Crosby
knew he was pretending to talk, and that no real sound
was issuing from his lips, the more he felt that he was

actually in conversation with himself. And it made him move even faster through the rain; knowing that he was a comfort to himself, and could make interesting conversation, entertain himself, even against the ugliest situations.

He said, "Ugly," and only once. He meant it about the weather, the tone of the sky. And not, oh shit no, about whatever was running him through the streets. At quarter to three Saturday morning.

The long street grew shorter as he approached the avenue that intersected it, and divided it from another seemingly endless crosstown city block. The rain stopped, and a light wind slowly whirled shallow puddles off the few awnings of stores and apartment buildings. A car would go by occasionally. A whore. One time a policeman watched Crosby from a doorway, lighting a cigarette. And probably wondered why this skinny little man was crying and shaking his head, working his jaws like speech, almost bulling up the deserted street. Crosby did break into a run occasionally, and usually when he did he would actually say some things. Usually he said, "Shit," or, "Goddamn goddamnit," clenching his teeth at the sound, his hands ripping away his jacket pockets, they were driven in so hard.

He had come, at 2:30 A.M., from a woman's house. A woman he had slept with many times. He had slept with her that night again. And when they had finished the action part of his visit, and the woman pulled his narrow body tightly against her own, he looked at his watch, which he hadn't taken off, and thought with a little start and maybe relief that he ought to be starting home. "It's two o'clock," he said to the woman. And she held him a little tighter, burying her face in his throat. "Leah, I've got to make it now."

The woman let him go suddenly, stretching one arm with its hand so they both hung awkwardly off the couch. That's where Crosby and Leah Purcell had been, for maybe an hour. Turning and grabbing on a narrow day-bed couch. Tearing each other's clothes, panting and pulling, till they both lay naked, or nearly naked, and now a little wasted, still shoved against each other so as not to fall off the narrow cot.

"You wouldn't stay all night?" Leah, on the outside, stretched one of her legs trying to get it solidly on the rug.

"I wouldn't. How could I?" Crosby pushed himself up on his hands. "How could I stay here all night?"

"I don't think you want to."

"No?"

"No. And besides, your wife wouldn't mind." The girl rolled completely away from him, putting both her feet on the floor. She ran her hand over a mound of clothes, trying to find her pants.

"No?"

"Hey, Lew." She got the pants and then the bras-siere. "Would you mind if Rachel were staying with somebody? No, I mean seeing somebody . . . like you do?"

Crosby pulled himself onto the floor and started to get his clothes together. He could do it more quickly than the girl, because even in the most fearful throes of passion he still knew exactly where he had thrown, or placed, his clothes. He started with his socks, and then his underwear. "What do you mean, seeing some-body?" His shirt, then the pants, fastening the belt. He took his tie out of the jacket.

Leah was still in her underwear. She stood now more in the center of the room, pulling her long hair together. "Suppose Rachel was seeing someone—sleeping with them—just like you and I sleep together, have been sleeping together, about twice a week for the last two months. Would it bother you?"

Lew smiled. He had his jacket on, and ran his hands through the pockets searching for cigarettes. When he got one in his mouth and knew that his speech would be muffled he half-shrugged half-didn't say some kind of affirmative answer. It meant yes though. And he even repeated it.

Leah stopped pulling her hair and bent down to-ward the floor to retrieve her large reddish comb. As she bent Lew squinted in the almost darkness, grimacing self-consciously at the woman's large self-conscious behind.

"It would, huh? It would really bother you . . . even though you do the same thing?"

"Uh huh." Lew took a step in the direction of the hall.

"What kind of thinking is that?"

"Mine." There was a book Lew came in with that he missed now, and he stooped to feel along the floor.

"Lew, don't go now. Stay for a while . . . let me make some tea. I've got some brandy too."

He got the book, and threw his raincoat over his shoulder. "Uh uh, I've got to make it."

"Oh, come on Lew, you don't have to go. Rachel won't mind. She's not even home."

A hot laugh dug through Lew Crosby's feelings, coming in through the nostrils and eyes. A good punch line. He was in the street and looking for money for a cab. But by the time it occurred to him to get a cab he had run almost thirteen blocks. A bunch of dominoes spilled over. Flap, flap, flap, etc., the white dots blinding him like monster streetlights. Flap, flap, flap. All kinds of recent history, in cold images ate at the white-hot screaming in his skin. The screaming he watched float up out of his stomach and scratch his eyeballs sideways. Now what? Now what? Now what? Or flap, flap flap, his steps, and legs, stretching out along the pavement. And his fiction still beat wet against his leg . . . flap flap flap.

At the house he stood a long time on the front step looking at the two front windows. It was dark inside. For sure For sure. And he had to put his head between his knees to cool the blood and nausea pumping at it from the inside. He put his hands on his hips, holding his head between his knees. Like a hurdler or half-miler. A bent wire squeezed together among the pictures. The stone tablets of conversation and act. He got days mixed up and dates, and stories. Fantasies replaced each other. Fantasies replaced realities. Realities did not replace anything. They were the least of anybody's worries. Even when he got inside and there was no one there. Or only the baby, sleeping very quietly in her crib, and an old college friend who had been staying at the house over the last few weeks.

Crosby walked up and down the long narrow apartment as if he were looking for clues. Even though he had gone through all the really vulgar Sherlock Holmes shit quite awhile ago. He came to the front then walked to the back. He did it again. And on the fourth trip to the front he shook Mickey Lasker on the couch, and spoke very rapidly to him at the moment Mickey opened his eyes. "Is Rachel at Mauro's house?"

Because Mickey was not quite awake he answered

immediately. "Yes . . . Yes . . . that's where she is." When he realized exactly what was happening, Lasker's eyes flew open and his hands fell and tightened at his sides. "Lew . . ." but Crosby had turned and run out of the house.

There was a light in Mauro's window. Or Lew figured at three o'clock it was probably the only window lighted. The loft was only a few blocks, about five, from Crosby's apartment. And the flaps then, thinking about the distance, fit a picture of something. For instance, "I'm going for a walk, Lew. I'll be back in a little while." Meaning, only five blocks, and not that brand of all-night magic. Finish *my* business while you read. And not with the cruelty it is to leave someone lying awake early mornings shuffling through faces.

Or "dance class," and a quick drink after, or stop in to hear some music, but home early, from jiving with the girls. (One of whom, "the girls," Lew found out, the wife of Crosby's closest friend, was fucking Mickey Lasker every chance she got. Mostly Thursdays . . . "dance" night.) "Oh, baby, it's Brook Farm." One of the things Lew pretended to say when the rain ran in his mouth.

But Rachel looked so quietly guilty, and it canceled what Lew thought when she came in on time from her screwing. Oh, come on asshole, don't make liars out of everybody. Or something, mixed with the slanting light on his book. The open bottle. His glass so handy, and plenty of good ideas. So fixed and necessary; that each thing remain understood. How can you read *Pierre* if you think your wife's doing something weird? Then you got to take time out to think about *her*. Oh boy . . . and then what? How much time can you waste like that? A poem? An honesty, like watching the rain from a doorway. Any simple but really complex way of feeling can be distorted by all these people. These conversations and rationales. Opinions, posturings, lies. Just to pass the time. From one dismal minute to the next. A bad painter sweeping his brush like counting. Talk, talk, talk (in a foreign accent). I don't want to say what I mean. But shutup anyway, I don't want to hear about you. Just live your life and shutup! Railing like that. Wasting every-thing. After it had taken so long to get it together. I am Lew Crosby, a writer. I want to write what I'm about, which is profound shit. Don't ask me anything. Just sit there if you want to. No, I'm not thinking. I'm just sit-ting. Don't try to involve yourself with me.

"Lew, Lew, answer me. Lew? Say, don't you ever lis-ten to what I'm saying?"

Now it wanted to rain again, just as Crosby opened the downstairs door. The loft was on the third floor. When he got outside the door he could hear low mu-sic and conversation. He banged on the door, almost as hard as he could. There was only more conversation, a little louder, but much the same as before. He didn't knock again, but the door swung open and he could see his wife sitting at a table just behind the short husky Japanese who opened the door.

"Hello, Lew," Mauro said, pulling the door wider. Crosby walked over to the table.

"Get your coat, Rachel." He wanted his voice to be soft and it almost was. "Get your coat and come on." His wife got halfway up from the table and looked over her shoulder.

"Lew," the painter said, "Lew, sit down and have a drink. We civilized people."

Crosby got hold of his wife's arm and pulled her out of the chair. He shoved her toward the door. The Japanese touched Crosby's arm.

"Lew, have a drink. We civilized people." Lew, of course, wanted to turn and hit Mauro in the face. Then he wanted to kick him in the face. But Mauro used to teach him, Lew, judo. Lew figured this clown just wanted to throw him on his ass. Wow. Brook Farm.

Lew got his wife's coat and pushed her through the door. She began to cry when they got to the bottom of the stairs. Lew wouldn't say anything. He walked a little in front of her. No rain now, only a damp sluggish wind off the river . . . and the spilling puddles. "Lew," Rachel was still crying, and louder. "Lew . . . Lew!" He walked faster, beginning to cross the wide avenue closest to their apartment. "Lew," Crosby's wife called very loudly, and he walked very quickly up the front steps.

He left the front door and the apartment door open. Rachel closed them as she passed. When she got inside the final door, Lew was standing in the middle of the room. Mickey Lasker brushed them both on the way out, tucking in his shirt. "Rachel," he just about whispered as he passed her.

"Lew," Rachel walked very close to her husband. The room was half-lit by a streetlight through a window, but also the sky was turning a little gray.

"You fucking whore. You goddamn fucking whore," Lew was looking out the window at the light. But he kept calling Rachel a fucking whore. She cried again, calling his name over and over. And he kept looking out the window repeating his thing. When Rachel touched his arm he spun around and swung at her hand. But then he started talking. "Why with that bastard? If you wanted to fuck somebody, why pick a complete dope? A stupid asshole like that? For chris'sake, for chris'sake. You know what? It follows all along . . . you just don't have any goddamn taste. A goddamn mediocrity. You were that when I first met you and goddamn you still are. A middle-class wreck. Christ, Christ . . . why don't you go the hell back where you came from? Christ. God!"

Her husband's stream of useless profanity cleared Rachel Crosby's head. She blew her nose while he shouted. And wiped her eyes. Lew went on shouting, but when he paused for a second Rachel said, as if she were holding a normal conversation, "What about you? What about you? I know you've been sleeping with Leah Purcell for the last few months. Nine o'clock in the morning. For God sakes! Lew, don't come on like that. How can you be so angry when you've been screwing around with that girl like you have? Leaving me here all the time. God, Lew . . . what did you expect?"

"I never slept with Leah Purcell." Lew was screaming now. Then he would shut up. Then he would call his wife a whore. Then he would call her mediocre, then he would say she needed a fool like Mauro because she was a fool. He wanted to call the Japanese a bad painter, but he figured that would be dumb. Even if it was true. "You're a dumb whore. A stupid mediocre bitch. Go away dumb whore. Go away."

He thrashed his arms, spit on the floor. Kicked tables and threw chairs against the wall. Smashed cheap glasses and pushed some flowers on the couch. Rachel started to scream now. All the things she'd said before. But now she screamed. And she hit her husband, on the chest and arms, till he stopped calling her a dumb whore, and began to grab at her arms. "I'll slap the hell out of you." He was trying to scream as loud as she was. She was saying go ahead . . . go ahead, and he slapped her once, across her face, and caught her before she fell. Then they stood holding each other for about thirty minutes.

*   *   *

When Lew pulled gently away from his wife it was even lighter in the room. He looked toward the front of the house and started walking toward the door. His wife said Lew again. But he left without speaking.

He almost retraced his steps. Not wobbling so much, but quickly, and only moving his mouth when he had something to say. When he got to the loft the light was dimmer but there was still a light. But now the downstairs door was locked. Lew brought up his hand stiffly and shoved it noisily through one of the door's small windows. Turning the knob from the inside he pushed the door open with his knee. There were three or four medium cuts on both sides of his hand, and they bled freely until Lew tied the hand in his handkerchief.

Once in the hall he leaped up the stairs, but as quietly as he could, landing on each step on his toes. When he got to Mauro's door his hand itched in the handkerchief and he remembered that the painter could probably wipe up the loft with him. So Crosby went back down one flight of stairs and rummaged through a pile of wood he remembered. But he took a metal pipe out of the pile and stuck it in his pocket with the cut-up hand.

When the door swung open this time Lew drew the pipe out and up and very hard down on Mauro's forehead. The next blow struck Rachel's lover near his ear. He fell quickly, with only a trifling wheeze. Blood was covering his head before he hit the floor.

Crosby looked at the man on the floor and still took a step into the room. He looked at the table with two separate crowds of beer cans. Then came in and looked at the unmade bed. He kneeled and smelled the wrinkled sheets. When he straightened up he tossed the pipe over his shoulder toward the painting area. Then he walked quickly through the door running down the stairs.

When the air hit him in the face, Lew got everything pretty straight. He even wondered whether the guy was dead. But he started, now, running in the street as fast as he could, twisting his hand up under a streetlight to see how badly it was hurt. He was running toward Leah Purcell's house.

* * *

About fifteen minutes later, running, walking, holding his hand at the wrist, or swinging it in wide arcs trying to stop it from stinging, Lew moved past the narrow tenement where Leah lived, and kept pushing down the street.

Seven o'clock he got to Bob Long's house, and some people were already hitting the street. Mostly Puerto Ricans, in sad vectors toward whatever ugly trick "Charlie" had put them in.

Another loft, with long shallow stairs. Bob lived at the top in a huge double studio with democratic antiques and his paintings. Blue girls, black girls, yellow and green girls. And in the background always some strange voyeur in a top hat riding a slow horse. Most of the paintings were that, or should have been that. Green people, orange people, magenta people. And they were always working out. Kama Sutra fashion. They made it from behind. Standing on horses. All ways. Girls and girls, men and horses. Girls and horses. And violent violet landscapes.

Inside, early early in the morning, Bob and two bohemians were getting ready to bolster the economy by sticking old needles in their arms. They greeted Lew, who was bleeding very badly, but only Bob got up to look at his hand. While he cleaned his hand Lew told Bob everything that had happened that night. Very quickly, like stage directions. Bob looked at him without saying anything. Letting Lew finish. They bandaged the hand. "Mauro, huh?" was all Bob would say. "Wow! Mauro, huh?"

"Yeh. I just left the cat. With his head caved in. I don't know if he's dead or not. I thought I'd sit around here for a while . . . you know."

"Yeh, man, yeh. Just sit." And then a soft benevolence came into Bob's voice. "Come on and get high with us. We got enough. And one of them turkeys can go get some more if we have to."

"What is it, horse?"

"Uh huh." Bob looked in the mirror at a mole on his chin. He ran some water in the sink and dabbed at the mole uselessly.

"I didn't know you did that."

"Oh, man, sure. Groovy stuff."

They went back to the nodding bohemians. Both of whom had taken as much out of the bag as they possibly could without making it 100 noticeable that they had gotten some of Bob's. Before he even looked at the bag Bob said, "O.K., which one of you faggots burned me?" Both of the bohemians laughed. "Eddie, you gonna have to make the run." Bob picked up the bag, shaking it and holding it up to the light. "Yeh, faggot, you better get on your horse."

Bob showed Lew what to do. And even put the needle into his arm. It was warm and dead in Lew's stomach throat and head. He sat so far away from anything you can name. Inside a deadness that kept so much uselessness away. Slow greedy pictures of dominoes.

Lew volunteered Eddie five dollars to make the run. Sitting with his knees hugged up under his chin; trying not to vomit, but harder and straighter anyway. And just out of everybody's reach.

Heroes Are Gang Leaders

My concerns are not centered on people. But in reflection, people cause the ironic tone they take. If I think through theories of government or prose, the words are sound, the feelings real, but useless unless people can carry them. Attack them, or celebrate them. Useless in the world, at least. Though to my own way of moving, it makes no ultimate difference. I'll do pretty much what I would have done. Even though people change me: sometimes bring me out of myself, to confront them, or embrace them. I spit in a man's face once in a bar who had just taught me something very significant about the socio-cultural structure of America, and the West. But the act of teaching is usually casual. That is, you can pick up God knows what from God knows who.

Sitting in a hospital bed on First Avenue trying to read, and being fanned by stifling breezes off the dirty river. Ford Madox Ford was telling me something, and this a formal act of teaching. The didactic tone of *No More Parades*. Teaching. Telling. Pointing out. And very fine and real in its delineations, but causing finally a kind of super-sophisticated hero worship. So we move from Tarzan to Christopher Tietjens, but the concerns are still heroism. And what to do to make the wildest, brightest dispersal of our energies. In our not really brief flight into darkness. Either it is done against the heavens, sky flyers, or against the earth. And the story of man is divided brusquely between those who know the sky, and those who know only the earth. And the various dictators, artists, murderers and ministers can come from either side. Each Left and Right, go right up to the sky, and the division is within their own territory. Lindberghs and Hemingways, Nat Turners and Robespierres. What they do is gold, and skyward, from whatever angle, they fly and return to an earth of mistakes. So Christopher Tietjens being made a cuckold, and trying vainly to see through mist and shadows down to Sylvia's earth. She called so furiously for him to fall. My friend, Johnny Morris, fighting off the Ku Klux Klan only to return from those heights to the silent hallway of some very real shack and watch some fool wrestle with his wife. Various scenes complete each other with desperate precision.

Sitting there being talked to by an old Tory, fixed and diseased by my only life. And surrounded, fortunately enough, by men like myself, who are not even able to think. Wood alcohol drinkers, dragged in from the Bowery, with their lungs and bellies on fire. Raving logicians who know empirically that Christianity can only take its place among the other less publicized concerns of men.

Sixty-year-old niggers who sit on their beds scratching their knees. Polacks who have to gurgle for the rest of their lives. Completely anonymous (Scotch-Irish?) Americans with dark ratty hair, and red scars on their stomachs. They might be homosexuals watching me read Thomas Me-an, and smelling the mystery woman's flowers. Puerto Ricans with shiny hair and old-fashioned underwear shirts, eating their dinner out of Mason jars.

And we are all alive at the same time. Contemporaries in that sense. (Though I still think myself a young man, and am still in love with things I can do.) Of the same time and source. Inheritors of so many things we will never understand. But weighted with very different allegiances, though if I am silent for a long time I hope we all believe in a similar reality. That I am not merely writing poems for Joel Oppenheimer or Paul Blackburn . . . but everything alive. Which is not true. Which is simply not true. Our heroisms and their claims are fictitious. But if we are not serious, if we do not make up a body of philosophy out of which to work we are simply hedonists, and I am stretching the word so that it includes even martyrs. Flame freaks.

In the bed next to mine was a man, Kowalski, a very

tall Polish man with a bony hairless skull, covered with welts and scratches. He had drunk paint remover and orange juice. He was the man who gurgled now, though he kept trying to curl his lips and smile. But I was hoping he would find out soon what a hopeless gesture that was, and stop it. I wanted to say to him, "Why don't you quit fucking around like that? It's certainly too late to be anybody else's man now. Just cut that shit out." With his weird colored teeth hanging below his lip, cutting the smile into strips of anguish.

He would eat my fruit when I offered it, or the nuts a rich lady gave me. Since I was not merely a "poor man" or a derelict, but a writer. That is, there was a glamorous reason I was in this derelict's ward. Look at my beard, and all the books on the table. I'm not like the rest of these guys. They're just tramps. But I'm a tramp with connections.

He would talk too, if I didn't watch him. He would gurgle these wild things he found in the tabloids. And point out murders and rapes to me, or robberies where everybody got away clean. He described the Bowery to me like it was a college, or the Village, or an artist's colony. An identical reality, with the same used up references . . . the same dishonesties and misplaced loyalties. The same ambition, naturally. Usually petty and ravaging. Another cold segment of American enterprise, and for this reason having nothing at all to do with their

European counterparts, beggars . . . whom I suppose
are academic and stuffy in comparison. Bums have the
same qualifications as any of us to run for president,
and it is the measure of a society that they refuse to.
And this is not romanticism, but simple cultural observation. Bums know at least as much about the world as
Senator Fulbright. You better believe it.

But one day two
men came into our ward. A tall red-faced man, like from
his neck up he had been painted by Soutine, or some
other nut. The other man was lost in his gabardine suit,
like somebody who was not even smart enough to be
rich. When I looked up from my book at them, I thought
immediately what a stupid thing to think about people
that they were cops. Although, of course, that is just
what they were: cops. Or detectives, since they were in
"plain" clothes, which is as hip as putting an alligator
in a tuxedo. Very few people would make a mistake,
except say those who would say it was a crocodile. That
is, zoology majors.

The alligators came right down the aisle to Kowalski's bed; the little baggy one carrying a yellow pad on a
writing board. They had been talking to each other very
calmly and happily about something. Probably about
man-eating tigers or the possibility of whores on Mars.
But their faces quickly changed and reset when they got
to the end of the row, and stood before my derelict's

bed. "Hey," the red-faced man said, "hey," at Kowalski who was sleeping or by now pretending to sleep, "Hey, you Kowalski?" He shook the old man's shoulder, getting him to turn over. Kowalski shook his head in imitation of sleep, frowned and tried to yawn. But he was still frightened. Probably confused too, since I'm sure he'd never expected to see cops in a place the Geneva Convention states very specifically is cool. In fact he wiped his eyes convinced, I'm certain, that the two police officers were only bad fairies, or at worst, products of a very casual case of delirium tremens. But, for sure, the two men persisted, past any idea of giggling fantasy.

"Hey. You Kowalski?"

The old man finally shook his head slowly yes, very very slowly, yes. Pulling his sheets up around his neck like a woman or an inventive fag, in a fit of badly feigned modesty. The cops looked on their list and back at Kowalski, the tall one already talking. "Where'd you get the stuff, Kowalski? Huh?" The derelict shrugged his shoulders and looked cautiously toward the window. "We wanna know where you got the stuff, Kowalski, huh?" Finally, it must have dawned on the derelict that his voice was gone. That he really couldn't answer the questions, whether he wanted to or not, and he gurgled for the men, and touched his throat apologetically. The red cop said, "Where'd you get the stuff, Kowalski, huh? Come on, speak up." And he put his head closer to the bum's, at the same time shaking his shoulder and finally, confronted by more gurgles, took the derelict's pajama shirt in his fingers and lifted the man a few inches off the bed. The little today man was alternately watching and listening, and making checks on his yellow pad. He said, "Comeon," once, but not very viciously; he looked at me and rubbed his eyes. "Comeon, fella."

The large cop raised his voice as he raised Kowalski off the bed, and shook him awkwardly from side to side, now only repeating the last part of the question, "Huh? Huh? Huh?" And the old bum gurgled, and began to slobber on himself, his face turning as red as the policeman's, and his eyes wide and full of a domesticated terror. He kept trying to touch his throat, but his arms were bent under his body, or maybe it was that he was too weak to raise them from where they hung uselessly at his side. But he gurgled and turned redder.

And here is the essay part of the story. Like they say, my *point of view*. I had the book *No More Parades*, all about the pursuit of heroism. About the death and execution of a skyman, or at least the execution, and the airless social compromise that keeps us alive past any use to ourselves. Chewing on some rich lady's candy, holding on to my ego, there among the elves, for dear god given sanctified life. Big Man In The Derelict Ward. The book held up in front of my eyes, to shield what was going on from slopping over into my life. Though, goddamn, it was there already. The response. The image. The total hold I had, and made. Crisscrossed and redirected for my own use (which now sits between the covers of a book to be misunderstood as *literature*. Like neon crosses should only be used to advertise pain. Which is total and final, and never really brief. It was all I had. Like Joe Friday, or César Vallejo, in a hopeless confusion of wills and intents. To be judged like Tietjens was or my friend in the hallway watching his wife or breaking his fingers against an automobile window. There is no reasonable attitude behind anything. Nuns, passion killers, poets, we should all go out and get falling down drunk, and forget all the rules that make our lives so hopeless. Fuck you Kowalski! Really, I really mean it. St. Peter doing his crossword puzzle while they wasted another hopeless fanatic. It fits, and is more logical than any other act. Ugly Polish tramp).

Till finally I said, "That man can't speak. His voice is gone."

And the tall man, without even looking, wheezed, "And who the fuck asked you?"

It is the measure of my dwindling life that I returned to the book to rub out their image, and studied very closely another doomed man's life.

The Screamers

Lynn Hope adjusts his turban under the swishing red green yellow shadow lights. Dots. Suede heaven raining, windows yawning cool summer air, and his musicians watch him grinning, quietly, or high with wine blotches on four-dollar shirts. A yellow girl will not dance with me, nor will Teddy's people, in line to the left of the stage, readying their *Routines*. Haroldeen, the most beautiful, in her pitiful dead sweater. Make it yellow, wish it whole. Lights. Teddy, Sonny Boy, Kenny & Calvin, Scram, a few of Nat's boys jamming long washed handkerchiefs in breast pockets, pushing shirts into homemade cummerbunds, shuffling lightly for any audience.

"The Cross-Over," Deen laughing at us all. And they perform in solemn unison a social tract of love. (With no music till Lynn finishes "macking" with any biglipped Esther screws across the stage. White and green plaid jackets his men wear, and that twisted badge, black turban/on red string conked hair. (OPPRESSORS!) A greasy hip-ness, down-ness, nobody in our camp be-

lieved (having social-worker mothers and postman fa-
thers; or living squeezed in lightskinned projects with
adulterers and proud skinny ladies with soft voices).
The theory, the spectrum, this sound baked inside their
heads, and still rub sweaty against those lesser lights.
Those niggers. Laundromat workers, beauticians, preg-
nant short-haired jail bait separated all ways from "us,"
but in this vat we sweated gladly for each other. And
rubbed. And Lynn could be a common hero, from whatever side we saw him. Knowing that energy, and its response. That drained silence we had to make with our
hands, leaving actual love to Nat or Al or Scram.

He stomped his foot, and waved one hand. The other
hung loosely on his horn. And their turbans wove in
among those shadows. Lynn's tighter, neater, and bright
gorgeous yellow stuck with a green stone. Also, those
green sparkling cubes dancing off his pinkies. A-boomp
bahba bahba, A-boomp bahba bahba, A-boomp bahba
bahba, A-boomp bahba bahba, the turbans sway behind
him. And he grins before he lifts the horn, at Deen or
drunk Becky, and we search the dark for girls.

Who would
I get? (Not anyone who would understand this.) Some
light girl who had fallen into bad times and ill-repute
for dating Bubbles. And he fixed her later with his
child, now she walks Orange St. wiping chocolate from
its face. A disgraced white girl who learned to calypso

in vocational school. Hence, behind halting speech, a humanity as paltry as her cotton dress. (And the big hats made a line behind her, stroking their erections, hoping for photographs to take down south.) Lynn would oblige. He would make the most perverted hopes sensual and possible. Chanting at that dark crowd. Or some girl, a wino's daughter, with carefully vase-lined bow legs, would drape her filthy angora against the cardboard corinthian, eying past any greediness a white man knows, my soft tyrolean hat, pressed cordu-roy suit, and "B" sweater. Whatever they meant, finally, to her, valuable shadows barely visible.

Some stuck-up boy with "good" hair. And as a na-ked display of America, for I meant to her that same oppression. A stunted head of greased glass feathers, orange lips, brown pasted edge to the collar of her dy-ing blouse. The secret perfume of poverty and ignorant desire. Arrogant too, at my disorder, which calls her smile mysterious. Turning to be eaten by the crowd. That mingled foliage of sweat and shadows: *Night Train* was what they swayed to. And smelled each other in The Grind, The Rub, The Slow Drag. From side to side, slow or jerked staccato as their wedding dictated. Big hats bent tight skirts, and some light girls' hair swept the resin on the floor. Respectable ladies put stiff arms on your waist to keep some light between, looking ner-vously at an ugly friend forever at the music's edge.

I wanted girls like Erselle, whose father sang on television, but my hair was not straight enough, and my father never learned how to drink. Our house sat lonely and large on a half-Italian street, filled with important Negroes. (Though it is rumored they had a son, thin with big eyes, they killed because he was crazy.) Surrounded by the haughty daughters of depressed economic groups. They plotted in their projects for mediocrity, and the neighborhood smelled of their despair. And only the wild or the very poor thrived in Graham's or could be roused by Lynn's histories and rhythms. America had choked the rest, who could sit still for hours under popular songs, or be readied for citizenship by slightly bohemian social workers. They rivaled pure emotion with wind-up record players that pumped Jo Stafford into Home Economics rooms. And these carefully scrubbed children of my parents' friends fattened on their rhythms until they could join the Urban League or Household Finance and hound the poor for their honesty.

I was too quiet to become a murderer, and too used to extravagance for their skinny lyrics. They mentioned neither cocaine nor Bach, which was my reading, and the flaw of that society. I disappeared into the slums, and fell in love with violence, and invented for myself a mysterious economy of need. Hence, I shambled anonymously thru Lloyd's, The Nitecap, The Hi-Spot,

and Graham's desiring everything I felt. In a new En-
glish overcoat and green hat, scouring that town for
my peers. And they were old pinch-faced whores full
of snuff and weak dope, celebrity fags with radio pro-
grams, mute bass players who loved me, and built the
myth of my intelligence. You see, I left America on the
first fast boat.

This was Sunday night, and the Baptists were still
praying in their "faboulous" churches. Though my father sat listening to the radio, or reading pulp cowboy
magazines, which I take in part to be the truest legacy
of my spirit. God never had a chance. And I would be
walking slowly toward The Graham, not even knowing how to smoke. Willing for any experience, any image, any further separation from where my good grades
were sure to lead. Frightened of post offices, lawyer's
offices, doctor's cars, the deaths of clean politicians. Or
of the imaginary fat man, advertising cemeteries to his
"good colored friends." Lynn's screams erased them all,
and I thought myself intrepid white commando from
the West. Plunged into noise and flesh, and their form
become an ethic.

Now Lynn wheeled and hunched himself for another tune. Fast dancers fanned themselves. Couples
who practiced during the week talked over their steps.
Deen and her dancing clubs readied *avant-garde* routines.
Now it was *Harlem Nocturne*, which I whistled loudly one

Saturday in a laundromat, and the girl who stuffed in my khakis and stiff underwear asked was I a musician. I met her at Graham's that night and we waved, and I suppose she knew I loved her.

Nocturne was slow and heavy and the serious dancers loosened their ties. The slowly twisting lights made specks of human shadows, the darkness seemed to float around the hall. Any meat you clung to was yours those few minutes without interruption. The length of the music was the only form. And the idea was to press against each other hard, to rub, to shove the hips tight, and gasp at whatever passion. Professionals wore jocks against embarrassment. Amateurs, like myself, after the music stopped, put our hands quickly into our pockets, and retreated into the shadows. It was as meaningful as anything else we knew.

All extremes were popular with that crowd. The singers shouted, the musicians stomped and howled. The dancers ground each other past passion or moved so fast it blurred intelligence. We hated the popular song, and any freedman could tell you if you asked that white people danced jerkily, and were slower than our champions. One style, which developed as Italians showed up with pegs, and our own grace moved toward bellbottom pants to further complicate the cipher, was the honk. The repeated rhythmic figure, a screamed riff, pushed in its insistence past music. It was hatred and frustration, secrecy and despair. It spurted out of the diphthong culture, and reinforced the black cults of emotion. There was no compromise, no dreary sophistication, only the elegance of something that is too ugly to be described, and is diluted only at the agent's peril. All the saxophonists of that world were honkers, Illinois, Gator, Big Jay, Jug, the great sounds of our day. Ethnic historians, actors, priests of the unconscious. That stance spread like fire thru the cabarets and joints of the black cities, so that the sound itself became a basis for thought, and the innovators searched for uglier modes. Illinois would leap and twist his head, scream when he wasn't playing. Gator would strut up and down the stage, dancing for emphasis, shaking his long gassed hair in his face and coolly mopping it back. Jug, the beautiful horn, would wave back and forth so high we all envied him his connection, or he'd stomp softly to the edge of the stage whispering those raucous threats. Jay first turned the mark around, opened the way further for the completely nihilistic act. McNeeley, the first Dada coon of the age, jumped and stomped and yowled and finally sensed the only other space that form allowed. He fell first on his knees, never releasing the horn, and walked that way across the stage. We hunched together drowning any sound, relying on Jay's contorted face for evidence that there was still music, though none of us needed it now. And then he fell backward, flat on his back, with both feet stuck up high in the air, and he kicked and thrashed and the horn spat enraged sociologies.

That was the night Hip Charlie, the Baxter Terrace Romeo, got wasted right in front of the place. Snake and four friends mashed him up and left him for the ofays to identify. Also the night I had the gray bells and sat in the Chinese restaurant all night to show them off. Jay had set a social form for the poor, just as Bird and Dizzy proposed it for the middle class. On his back screaming was the Mona Lisa with the mustache, as crude and simple. Jo Stafford could not do it. Bird took the language, and we woke up one Saturday whispering *Ornithology*. Blank verse.

And Newark always had a bad reputation, I mean, everybody could pop their fingers. Was hip. Had walks. Knew all about The Apple. So I suppose when the word got to Lynn what Big Jay had done, he knew all the little down cats were waiting to see him in this town. He knew he had to cook. And he blasted all night, crawled and leaped, then stood at the side of the stand, and watched us while he fixed his sky, wiped his face. Watched us to see how far he'd gone, but he was tired and we weren't, which was not where it was. The girls rocked slowly against the silence of the horns, and big hats pushed each other or made plans for murder. We had not completely come. All sufficiently eaten by Jay's memory, "on his back, kicking his feet in the air, Go-ud Damn!" So he moved cautiously to the edge of the stage, and the gritty Muslims he played with gathered close. It was some mean honking blues, and he made no attempt to hide his intentions. He was breaking bad. "Okay, baby," we all thought, "go for yourself." I was standing at the back of the hall with one arm behind my back, so the overcoat could hang over in that casual gesture of fashion. Lynn was moving, and the camel walkers were moving in the corners. The fast dancers and practicers making the whole hall dangerous. "Off my suedes, motherfucker." Lynn was trying to move us, and even I did the one step I knew, safe at the back of the hall. The hippies ran for girls. Ugly girls danced with each other. Skippy, who ran the lights, made them move faster in that circle on the ceiling, and darkness raced around the hall. Then Lynn got his riff, that rhythmic figure we knew he would repeat, the honked note that would be his personal evaluation of the world. And he screamed it so the veins in his face stood out like neon. "Uhh, yeh, Uhh, yeh, Uhh, yeh," we all screamed to push him further. So he opened his eyes for a second, and really made his move. He looked over his shoulder at the other turbans, then marched in time with his riff, on his toes across the stage. They followed; he marched across to the other side, repeated, then finally he descended, still screaming, into the crowd, and as the sidemen followed, we made a path for them around the hall. They were strutting, and all their horns held very high, and they were only playing that one scary note. They moved near the back of the hall, chanting and swaying, and passed right in front of me. I had a little cup full of wine a murderer friend of mine made me drink, so I drank it and tossed the cup in the air, then fell in line behind the last wild horn man, strutting like the rest of them. Bubbles and Rogie followed me, and four-eyed Moselle Boyd. And we strutted back and forth pumping our arms, repeating with Lynn Hope, "Yeh, Uhh, yeh, Uhh." Then everybody fell in behind us, yelling still. There was confusion and stumbling, but there were no real fights. The thing they wanted was right there and easily accessible. No one could stop you from getting in that line. "It's too crowded. It's too many people on the line!" some people yelled. So Lynn thought further, and made to destroy the ghetto. We went out into the lobby and in perfect rhythm down the marble steps. Some musicians laughed, but Lynn and some others kept the note, till the others fell back in. Five or six hundred hopped-up woogies tumbled out into Belmont Avenue. Lynn marched right in the center of the street. Sunday night traffic stopped, and honked. Big Red yelled at a bus driver, "Hey, baby, honk that horn in time or shut it off!" The bus driver cooled it. We screamed and screamed at the clear image of ourselves as we should always be. Ecstatic, completed, involved in a secret communal expression. It would be the form of the sweetest revolution, to huckle-buck into the fallen capital, and let the oppressors lindy hop out. We marched all the way to Spruce, weaving among the stalled cars, laughing at the dazed white men who sat behind the wheels. Then Lynn turned and we strutted back toward the hall. The late show at the National was turning out, and all the big hats there jumped right in our line.

Then the Nabs came, and with them, the fire engines. What was it, a labor riot? Anarchists? A nigger strike? The paddy wagons and cruisers pulled in from both sides, and sticks and billies started flying, heavy streams of water splattering the marchers up and down the street. America's responsible immigrants were doing her light work again. The knives came out, the razors, all the Biggers who would not be bent, counterattacked or came up behind the civil servants smashing at them with coke bottles and aerials. Belmont writhed under the dead economy and splivs floated in the gutters, disappearing under cars. But for a while, before the war had reached its peak, Lynn and his musicians, a few other fools, and I still marched, screaming thru the maddened crowd. Onto the sidewalk, into the lobby, halfway up the stairs, then we all broke our different ways, to save whatever it was each of us thought we loved.

Salute

It started when I was coming up North Gun Road on my way from the flight line back to my barracks. Bright and hot afternoon, in Puerto Rico. The heavy engines scraping the heat down heavier. Overhead the big planes pulled their noses up, or dipped them coming across the flat blue water, clearing thick palms, the town of San Locas, the long high metal fence, then down, if the pilot was good on most of the wheels, down onto the long flat runway, the engines churning and spinning metallic light across the tar and cement. When planes left or came in, you'd turn your head, no matter how many times, just to watch. Maybe only a few seconds. But watch, till the thing disappeared on the ground, to be wheeled close to a hangar by the grease balls, or off and up, like into the sun, out across the motionless sky.

I was walking slowly, or pretty slowly, in shabby two-piece fatigues, the kind with the color washed out. My fatigue hat was the same color, the brim frayed and bent so the edges fit down tight around my eyes. My stripes . . . there were two of them . . . bent at the edges away from the cloth of the fatigues, old soldier style, though I was only maybe a year and a half in, with another year and a half to go.

The air force was where I did all my reading, or a great deal of it. At least it was where I started coming on like a fullup intellectual, and got silent and cagey with most of the troops, and stayed in my room most nights piling through *Ulysses* or Eliot or something else like that. Sometimes writing shreds of literature myself, most times about things of which I had very little knowledge at all. Death or Eternity or Love or something like that, weeping sometimes at my fate, hitched like a common fool (I'd come up with the word Plebeian a few days before, and used it to insult my duty sergeant who just retorted by doubling my duties. And he didn't even know what the hell I was saying . . . though he asked one lieutenant later in the day, who told him . . . and of course the man felt more than justified piling it on me, who was, besides being an insufferable silent snob, a loose-mouth nigger . . . both at the same time) to the air force of the united states. Weep was what I did then, not even really, those long nights, being actually hurt. I was bugged maybe, but the thought of weeping was what animated me. It was deep and got me into a zone of feeling I'd only guessed existed before. Once really in college I walked up Georgia Avenue pretending to be a faggot, feeling alone and weeping in my hands. That was for effect. No it was a dull night in the dormitory, and the hopelessness of the thing, the circumstance, maybe, of being locked off the streets, by the foreignness of the city, Washington, D.C., and the inequitable foreignness of my own changing insides, drove me out, even against my will, onto those streets which revolved slowly in the fog like moors. But those were solid beginnings, or maybe the affair was older than that anyway, there are hundreds of halfway houses to any revelation, and the simplest fact of vision needs probably hundreds of seeings.

Tears then were harder because the social context was more normal, that is, outwardly, college feeling, the twists of late adolescence are everywhere advertised as American phenomena anyone should understand. The army thing is too though, through the endless happiness of a Sad Sack or Marion Hargrove, or the Jewish soldier, Sam Levene, and the good strong cowboy, who are bosom buddies and whichever survives will in fact weep himself, over his friend's body, hugging the dead flesh to his face, with the shells and enemy bursting all around this suddenly understandable passion. I remember seeing even a few intellectuals, shambling stupidly through their agonizing paces, the meaninglessness and essential cowardice of thought being everywhere evident at least to anyone who watched the thin four-eyed

dope who covered the real world with words that im-
pressed the producer's mother.

But this real army life was, like any reality, duller,
less flashy than any kind of fancy, and finally a lot grim-
mer. So the quality of response, and observation. I'd read
all day when I could, or walk down near the beaches.
I'd read all night if nobody came in to talk or with an
open jug of rum, and similar sad nostalgias. (These
from my few friends, other fledgling thinkers and lost
geniuses of feeling.) In those days we were finding out
things wholesale, there was so much we didn't know
that could be picked up even from the Sunday Times,
the air mail copy of which cost seventy-five cents, since
it was flown down from the States Saturday night to
keep all the colonists happy. I made lists of my reading,
with critical comments that grew more pompous with
each new volume, even my handwriting changed and
developed a kind of fluency and archness that wanted
to present itself as sophistication. I made my own fric-
tions. I sent my own brain out into any voids I imagined
I could handle. Actual trips into San Locas for whores
and all-night drunks were kept to a minimum, since the
projection of any despair I felt to be my own responsibility, and wanted such revelation orderly, or at least
completely at my beck and call. I wanted to cry when I
wanted to cry, in this sense, like any big businessman,
loving only those accidents that I could use positively.

So the urge to walk around dark waterfronts or hang out with ancient sex deviates or share the whore's bed with two other soldiers, I kept to as few requests as possible. And just one deathly trip through the off limits venereal disease capital of the island, hotly pursued by pimps and their hunchbacked wives, who waved their knives and cursed what they thought was an America I loved, would suffice for weeks . . . since I felt then for the first time in my life, that words were equally as dangerous, or at least I knew they could set the blood flowing in my face as quickly as the stale breath of any Puerto Rican.

But the only real thing reading does for anyone is to shut them up for a few hours, and let the other senses function as usefully as the mouth. Quiet already, a young man will grow sullen. Sullen, he will grow into stone. But any "normal" most times noisy city half-slick young college type hipster will close his mouth for all times, so ugly will have been the nature of his re-evaluation of the world, and his life.

So the service became my first arena. The ideas that were coming in so quickly (in Chicago a few months earlier I had made a vow to myself that every day I would learn something . . . that afternoon I began to read *Ulysses*) I tried to implement immediately, although most times, I was so unsure as to what they were exactly, as life things, that I must have carried a very heavy frustration around with me like a gun. Side streets were tunnels into myself, on all those cold days. Nights would open me up, or twist my insides out, so that the blood of my desire flowed on sidewalks and even, naturally enough, into gutters. Chicago was the town I went through the most changes in. I slept with a couple of old women . . . or maybe only one of them was really old. She had some name that suggested the church to me. (Remembering, now, Lorca, and his understanding of the sexual basis to the Spanish Catholic church: Martyrs staggering toward that specifically Spanish heaven, the bodies full of arrows, blood shining, because of the painter's mind, and the sun drawn with wide yellow staffs to portray it as divine. Spanish wars too, thick with deep greens and purples, popeyed diers strangling on their horses, death everywhere, beautiful laceration of the world.) And that was more guilt, if that's really what it is that holds me so firmly to the world. At any rate I thought then, even so young, and still maintain that it is simple guilt that makes me move at all. Only feeling comes to me, and did then, plain and unexplainable.

Without a thought, then, I walked around that desert, and held my screams in check. Most times in reverie like dilettante *petit mal*. There were holes in the world. Holes everywhere. I filled them with whatever I could find. My pain, or laughter, secret learnings, and staring hours at my face, picking shaving bumps, in the mirror.

But now there was a thin blond man standing directly in front of me. He didn't know me. He'd never even seen me before. (Maybe his mother got fucked by an escaped mad coon sex deviate who resembled the perspiration of my ideas. Or the father? I mean, there could have been some wild connection . . . did his wife buy a broom in my grandfather's grocery store? No. In the South or the North? Ahhh. No she never been there.

But now there was a thin blond man standing directly in front of me. He didn't know me. He'd never even seen me before. (Maybe . . . but he recognized the clothes I wore, though he didn't like their style. He wdn't now, with what I've got on this minute, yellow corduroy pants, and a beard, so no progress finally.

He recognized I was in the service same as him, only he was thin blond stupidly stern, and he required a service of me. A duty. He watched me I suppose move past him, with story wind blinding me. I didn't see the cat, really. Or maybe I did, and figured I'd dreamed him, and wanted to dissolve him to get back to the part of the bit where I go down on the tall black girl in the swamps.

"You in a hurry, Airman?" I heard. He recited the Magna Charta and Bill of Rights before I turned without moving to see him as he rode in with the afternoon, hot and alien. "You in a hurry?" What hurry would I be in? I had, I think I said, another year and a half in this shit. Where would I be going? I didn't know. I wondered did this cat really have something important to say. But he was a lieutenant. First or second, and maybe from Baltimore or Wilmington. A place nobody has to think about, except for the ugly edge of South in his speech.

"What's the matter with you?" I heard. He tried to remember Joe Dimaggio's consecutive game streak, his mother's face, the key to his happiness, with fifty bucks a minute in a clean town near the Gulf. Shit, he was a human being too.

"Don't you know you're supposed to salute officers?" I heard. He might almost have grinned if I hadn't looked so evil. But that's the way I look all the time. Check my fan club pictures and see. All autographed "With Emotional Prestige . . . All Best . . . Ray Robinson." But I cdn't tell him that then. I thought he wdn't understand . . . that's the kind of prick I was.

When the focus returned. (Mine) I don't know what that means. Focus, returned . . . that's not precise enough. Uh . . . I meant, when I could finally say something to this guy . . . I didn't have anything to say. But I knew that in the first place. I said, "Yes sir, I know all about it." No, I didn't say any such shit as that. I sd, "Well, if the airplanes blow up, Chinese with huge habits will drop out of the sky, riding motorized niggers." You know I didn't say that. But I said something, you know, the kind of shit you'd say, you know.

Words

Now that the old world has crashed around me, and it's raining in early summer. I live in Harlem with a baby shrew and suffer for my decadence which kept me away so long. When I walk in the streets, the streets don't yet claim me, and people look at me, knowing the strangeness of my manner, and the objective stance from which I attempt to "love" them. It was always predicted this way. This is what my body told me always. When the child leaves, and the window goes on looking out on empty walls, you will sit and dream of old things, and things that could never happen. You will be alone, and ponder on your learning. You will think of old facts, and sudden seeings which made you more than you had bargained for, yet a coward on the earth, unless you claim it, unless you step upon it with your heavy feet, and feel actual hardness.

Last night in a bar a plump black girl sd, "O.K., be intellectual, go write some more of them jivey books," and it could have been anywhere, a thousand years ago, she sd, "Why're you so cold?" and I wasn't even thinking coldness. Just tired and a little weary of myself. Not even wanting to hear me thinking up things to say.

But the attention. To be always looking, and thinking. To be always under so many things' gaze, the pressure of such attention. I wanted something, want it now. But don't know what it is, except words. I cd say anything. But what would be left, what would I have made? Who would love me for it? Nothing. No one. Alone, I will sit and watch the sun die, the moon fly out in space, the earth wither, and dead men stand in line, to rot away and never exist.

Finally, to have passed away, and be an old hermit in love with silence. To have the thing I left, and found. To be older than I am, and with the young animals marching through the trees. To want what is natural, and strong.

Today is more of the same. In the closed circle I have fashioned. In the alien language of another tribe. I make these documents for some heart who will recognize me truthfully. Who will know what I am and what I wanted beneath the maze of meanings and attitudes that shape the reality of everything. Beneath the necessity of talking or the necessity for being angry or beneath the actual core of life we make reference to digging deep into some young woman, and listening to her come.

Selves fly away in madness. Liquid self shoots out of the joint. Lives which are salty and sticky. Why does everyone live in a closet, and hope no one will understand how badly they need to grow? How many errors they canonize or justify, or kill behind? I need to be an old monk and not feel sorry or happy for people. I need to be a billion years old with a white beard and all of ASIA to walk around.

The purpose of myself has not yet been fulfilled. Perhaps it will never be. Just these stammerings and poses. Just this need to reach into myself, and feel something wince and love to be touched.

The dialogue exists. Magic and ghosts are a dialogue, and the body bodies of material, invisible sound vibrations, humming in emptyness, and ideas less than humming, humming, images collide in empty ness, and we build our emotions into blank invisible structures which never exist, and are not there, and are illusion and pain and madness. Dead whiteness.

We turn white when we are afraid.

We are going to try to be happy.

We do not need to be fucked with.

We can be quiet and think and love the silence.

We need to look at trees more closely.

We need to listen.

Harlem 1965

New-Sense

Nothing changed in the passage. The same world. The same decisions. Only the role is altered, the "facing up." Shadows stalk the same. Sounds hang. The hand on the face, knees bent to sit, quiet a fitful thing, and the honest people somehow cowed because they want to say so much filth on themselves, they cannot focus on the filth of their enemies.

I lived in a small town, and grew up in a small town. I lived in large cities, and was small-town in the midst of them. I lived in big mansions that were small shacks huddled against the screams of the poor. I lived fantasies in the center of ugly reality. And reality was the feeling I wanted, and escaped to, from a fantasy world, where I cd have everything. Where I cd be everything.

O.K., let it focus on women. My typing and thinking are slow after so long a layoff my fingers and the fingers of this skyscraper I carry around on my neck. But who can be involved in anything like screaming passion? Except your dick gets hard, and you want to hug somebody to it. You want some warmth. You want to lay back and look at the ceiling, and smoke grass and relax away from yr tedious ambitions.

Gray romance. On and on. It comes again. Like after the sudden summer, being jammed up in a room talking shakespeare at night w/ a white girl, and then going for that for the difference it made. The slight difference, which is no slightness, but a narrow turning that pushed on, means you have arrived at a different place. A different world.

But there was no burning screaming menace involved. No passion. Except the pushing and wondering if this was really the way beautiful things happened. The logic and rationales we posited. The sucking and licking. The turning and lying. The need to have each other, and be different for that.

But essentially you find yrself w/ someone and that's that. Unless some heavy thing can shake you. Or you're just an ambling hunk of swine and bone, just poking along, rejecting this vegetable, or eating all of them, making thick layers of dead rot we must call our kindest memories. Our sentiment.

But unless you think about it, focus on it, romance is dream. And what is with you is gray dull heavy. Tho it can lead to the deepest flash connection. And the spiritual value of looking up in the dim quiet and seeing the same face is an umbrella of God. Why we feel so deeply things might possibly be "organized."

You can either sit and think about what you're doing, which is then nothing at all. Or move, and faster, and faster, and zooooom, not even maybe get the chance to feel what's happening. Nothing in private, nothing to think about, since it's all presented, and there, and present to be talked about, and murdered over. No reflection.

Dull romance. What life can finally be. What you sit and remember, and what you do, the really scorching part of everything, so fast it goes without you, though it has you in it.

What we produce leads back to ourselves. Input-transducer-Output. And from the last we know something of the machine that produced it. All accident and passion, or the black man in black or the white man in white, feeding variables into a known piece of machinery.

(O world I want to change you, and these fantasies are sundays in the wet silence, gathering my strength about me, clear and free, for a hard thing. Which must be done, and gotten, in order that peace come, and be free, and unconditional.)

* * *

We would be in love now. I could go make love to somebody right now, instead of hacking at this machine. Right now, lost second, I could. And pull them close to me, and be said to find and be in, LOVE. But there's a kind of raw thin quality to it. A slotting. That I'm reacting to. A fixity and predictability to myself, in that context that holds me away. Even tho the context itself can never be predicted. (Unless yr abstract white man sitting with sequined beasts.

Their teeth. Their smiling. Shit it turns yr stomach.)

That close thing is always valuable. And only sick people want to speculate about it. Want to see it. When you can't see it. Nothing to see, except the voyeur bullshit, a kind of distorted diseased intellectualism.

But it's the same thing. Wanting to understand what's going on, rather than just getting in it moving. Like Jake and Ray in my man's book. Jake moved straight and hard and survived with a fox in Chicago, probably, where he'd come home tired and drunk at nights after work and work this happiness over (her name was Felice). And Ray, a name I'd already saved for my self, sailing around the stupid seas with a "wistful" little brown girl waiting for him while he masturbated among pirates . . . dying from his education. Shit. It's too stupid to go into.

Can we make a world and do actual work in it? Can

we find actual love in it? Everything. What provides the slim inch of satisfaction in life?

(But that's the point, "Satisfaction." What is that? Hulme spoke of "Canons of Satisfaction." He meant a hierarchy of what grooves you.

And what we try to do. Not try. The thinkers try. The extremists, Confucius says, shooting past the mark. But the straight ahead people, who think when that's what's called for, who don't when they don't have to. Not the Hamlet burden, which is white bullshit, to always be weighing and measuring and analyzing, and reflecting. The reflective vs. the expressive. Mahler vs. Martha and the Vandellas. It's not even an interesting battle.

Except we black people caught up in Western values. So deeply. Having understood the most noble attempts of white men to make admirable sense of the world, now, reject them, along with any of them. And the mozarts are as childish as the hitlers.

Because reflect never did shit for any of us. Express would. Express. NOW NOW NOW NOW NOW NOW.

Blood Everywhere.
And heroes march thru
smiling.

Unfinished

Coming into Jocks in Harlem, with friends and the inside redlit up middle-class faggots (no, homosexuals) scattered discreetly around, sharp in their new shit.

Summer evening, with friends, I said. Their faces float around, and their names. Love, talk, expectation, the leading on. The close light that separates the tribes of life. Where is the spectacular, and the handling of it, and the love of it, and the reward for its being alive and screaming? The love of everything.

Which is calm enough. These faces hanging in the calm, and the low talk and occasional soft ha-ha of a fag.

Then you sprawl and talk about what happened that day, that wild summer 65 uptown, when a lot new blood came in, and there were a lot of closer questioners of day to day making-it in America.

The atmosphere is important. Very important. The tales people will tell even to this day, of shit that simply did not happen. Feet walked by above us. You cd see some through a window. Few people made up biographies for them.

There were snakes and panthers in the town. Tho a lot of funny shit happened. A lot of fools got exposed. A lot of cowards. A lot of maniacs. Reality syndrome. Black people piled in the street. Negroes piled in certain nigger coolout stations.

WHITE PHILANTHROPY RUNS AMUCK AGAIN

Sit in a useless evening not even getting drunk. Just with people and make some remarks. Maybe these dancers were there that night, and there was nothing to talk about because you can't talk to dancers about academic shit like what the world is. So you can suck-sipping ale out the end of a glass, listen to some vague shit about somebody who told somebody else off, and not even be there. You could be in southcarolina murdering the governor, by strangling him with a wide belt, and your knee cocked in the small of his back.

People are going about their business. Somebody else comes in the bar, everybody looks up, the fags respond or disrespond, or if it's somebody somebody knows, there is a little more racket, before the half-white juke box takes over again. And maybe some lightskinned lady with streaks in her hair will wander in mission unknown.

All settled in time and space, another nothing to

add to hundreds of others. The various freaks up and down the streets. Like black blondes or niggers with good jobs. Maybe junkies from southcarolina who came up north to get deadhooked forever, in the evil smells of dying blackness. But they, at least, are real. These dead junkies. In their weird outside world. But then another colored man will stop in the hallways of some shaky white philanthropy and talk to you like he was practicing to be a traitor.

A multiplicity of failures. But everybody, shit, can claim something. To have made it! Whatever. From whatever to where ever the wind blows enough dollars to cool out bad conscience. Facing us, on the street each day, thousands of fools and cowards.

So they all join hands and make a fool/coward cartel that controls the minds of ordinary men. And it is this cartel we work against, to kill them. Drown them in their blood, so that the mind might again soar to its completion and a new brightness begin.

We could sit and joke, or if with heavier friends, philosophize about the day, Malcolm's death, the number of faggots in The Big Apple, being careful not to offend anybody sitting in our immediate party.

And simple bullshit incidents lend a personal form to time. And all the facts we want are carried back with the specific context of their happening.

Red bar faces. The room tilted under the ground, just a few steps down. The gaiety of pretension. These creeps won't even get like in the Harlem Club, and tear the windows out. These are cool Knee Grows who have a few pesos in their pockets (earned by letting whitey pass gas in their noses). There is a cruel frustration drifts through places like that . . . places filled with young & old black boushies . . . And you could think about white invisible things being dragged back and forth across the ceiling. Maybe they are talismans of white magic, secret, hideous, ofay mojos, their god waves back and forth over black people's heads, making them long to be white men. It's too horrible to think about shit like that.

This kind of thing can be entertaining or no. But it's always intimidating.

A guy came into this bar, probably just stopped raining outside. Very light sprinkle. And this guy comes in hooked up in these weird kind of metal crutches, where they have metal straps around the legs. A kind of big brown cat, bulky even strapped and crippled up like he was. He was making some kind of noise when he came into the place. Or it was some kind of rumble accompanied him in, limping like he was on those metal rods. He must been at the bar 10 seconds before he pulls himself over near our table. Metal niggers slid out of his way. I was not even looking.

But it wasn't me anyway. I'm here writing, this never happened to this person. It was somebody else.

At the table sitting watching him approach the friends of the world, all happy at being that. No, these shitty dancers, with lyrical eyelashes, and little tiny walks if they're technically male, just barely women. The women, the same, only it's not as spectacular to be women invert like it is for men. The burden of balls.

Oh the weird smiles that exist in life. Too much. To think about right now, but if you ever get a chance think about that shit. How many different kinds of smiles there are, and what they infer or imply or telegraph.

When the cripple cat came up to the table he says some shit to one of the guys. Like he had seen him the other night on television. And the guy who had been congratulated for being on television gave a sort of pseudo-humble hero smile (which is not a rare variety actually).

Yes, yes, yes (addressing the people in invisible dreams). Yes, yes, that is my work, yes, oh wow, groove somebody recognized he and set up the guillotine trap. A long terrorized scream, and the blade, bloody already comed whistling down. Trying to smile at people is experimentation or cliché. I have a standard good natural tooth viewer I use most times in such occasions. But was that me at the table. The one who speaks now. The heart that feeds me my life.

But this is a story now. There are facts in it anyway, for the careful.

This was a funny looking guy, he needed to stop smiling so you could get a good look at his face. But that's probably why he kept smiling . . . a really fucking sinister smile . . . now that I think about it. Or maybe not sinister, but insinuating, dangerous by default.

And keeps talking and talking, ordering drinks. He began doing this the minute he got up to the table. And fairly loud getting louder with each click of my machine. He was very loud by now. And laughing. But the laughter was decoration for something colder than you ever ran into.

Yeh I saw you on television, and you gave em hell boy. L the minute I saw that program I wanted to call up the station and tell them crackers how much I agreed with what you were saying. Hand. Hand. Pats—shakes. Smiles. Crackers. Honkies. All the words. I was watching. L was watching like he does, close up and steady, big deep eyes to see. And seeing, can you act my man, the question hung in the world hot as sun. But sunshine is cool, ain't it? It grows the shit from in my heart. It makes the earth magic start. It's cool, and beauty, ba-by. Ba-by. Everything is all right. Up tight. Out of sight. Went on and on, warm lights glows walk box walk.

Be lady fair sister sliding down bars, Through Wars, and smoke of dead niggers, negroes, coons, woogies, etcetera, killing each other. Killing Each Other. Selves. Selves. Killing Each Other.

> I heard your thing,
> can you dig mine. You
> a success in the West,
> aint that a mess. Up in
> your ches' Polluted
> Stream. Dead fish,
> animals still to evolve.
> A fluke, like black and
> white together in the
> same head or bed, it
> makes no never mind.

He came at me, H had tied my hands behind me, got me in the face. It was bad, and blood came out.

> Where. TimeGap
> keys. Senseless
> Strung Gulls low
> over the sea. That
> was another
> incident in the
> spanish lowlands
> with Hannibal's
> mulattoes, still
> passing for White.

But yall cain'
fight.

Correction. The above is bullshit twisted from another time.

What happened. He was bleeding his twisted love. Like the story, and the image of piles of dead fish being broken in half by a jew to feed niggers at the seashore. Shure Rastus. We miss understand, by 3 and one half inches.

Bleed is it bleed bleed bleed. Love, they want white love and there's nothing like that in the world. There's no white peace either (Oh you mis understand . . . we sd *Peach* . . . simple colored monarch. "Arrest Him For Sodomy . . . He Fucked Melville." I'm in jail listening to the cripple now. He moaning inside he loves you so. Stand up L. He wants to touch you his mouth is close, with Vat 69 breath stinging your pause. He got pause thass why he teach moles to shit outta airplanes.

He was going to hit L. He loved him so much. He was going to hit. Him. Why he was screaming inside. Inside. Where the true song rages forever like the very sun. Inside he was screaming it was me not you you just said it but it was me I live and am hurt by the mother-fucking world so deeply, much deeper than you what the fuck do you know what the motherfucking shit do you know frail ass motherfucker i'm a cripple hurt motherfucker you ever feel 10 thousand passion tender notes eat your face for time.

He raged now, dropping his crutches on the floor. Inside flowed on out. It was out fire down below, all in the street, fags look out, the cripple, a giant of a man, a motherfucker . . . WATCH OUT L . . . WATCH

And L, cool, said brother, what you in to?

The cat came back from outside. He had another drink he came back over. Aw I aint into shit man. I used to sing my ass off though. He began singing. Something about love naturally. A song faggotass Tony Bennett used to sing. But this cat was singing about an actual kingdom, of kings and queens. And he disappeared smiling into the night.

New Spirit

I sprung my face and the brains fell out. I saw this little girl. I was sitting thinking about the time the plumber came, I paid him and he didn't do anything. I was in the basement, looking up at cold morning. My face was leaking, the furnace fire grumbled and I wanted to re-member this story, a tale, to tell you, miss, before you left to ride the invisible flesh of the world.

They were sitting talking about you, Bumi. About stuff they wanted you to be, and think, about an image they had of eating potato salad and going to the girl-friends. A cross around your neck. My face was covered with hot brains. They made a talk-noise, and the people thought it was me. Hello, Bumi, you still there, still hear me??

They wanted to be angry. Your mother frowned and murmured Christia like it was something she knew about knew, in fact, a christ-jew a beatnik in sandals with a psychedelic twitch. He seed stuff.

We beat drums through the talk. We beat drums. We chanted to you, baby, wanted you back. Nothing.

But they said god was white and you could see him in the chapel of the unity funeral home, waiting for funerals. The undertaker was a stereotype nigger faggunder, taker. He was taking me, baby. Caskets start at . . . he went on picking his soul's nose.

Your mother knew that thinking killed you. It made you worry. She had no use for it. She probably right, baby. The shit I put on you. But not no wooden cross to carry. I wanted a woman. I needed the shelter of someone's arms, and there you were. My friend Jr. Walker put it thus.

Then the next day they wanted to know whether or not I was going to steal the baby clothes. The furnace of flowers around you. The silent bed. Your sandals. Your stepping rhythms pulling my skin apart, they wanted to know if I was going to give your clothes back.

See that's what makes you paranoid, people saying shit like that. And being right among logs, and letters, toads never changing, the mist around that birth spot, where they settle into mud, returned, wait you can't unebolve (v don't exist for us) but there they go, back in the water.

Ceremony: Middleclass negroes
           Yoruba temple
           Nationalists
           Inch of Hippy
           Where was I? Why didn't I go?

I was there, love, listening to these people in the front room discuss the night in the hospital when they discussed the night in the front room. Serj can verify this. The night she came to me, in front of a burning building, and we invaded the starroads. And the other woman. And the other woman. And the long black sister she took. The other woman. We weep together. She is not asking me the same questions. She is floating against the sides of the room, being looked at, deciding, whether she wants to be a colored woman. You didn't have the choice baby, the way you came in, straight off the warm streets, straight into the future.

Now I'm getting something together to say to them to yr people, all of them. I want you when you want me again. We'll get together, hang out or something. Even your shadow has split. Nothing here but dumb shit, and me.

You want to talk to this cat called me from newyork with the white wife, no, i mean with somebody else's white wife?? No. You want to speak to Sandy or Linda or Moosey or Bobby, or JB or that fat little girl with the big behind? The peace lady? O.K., I'll tell them what you sd.

In the hospital the people didn't seem disturbed, they told jokes. We just don't realize how many people die. (You cd ride a bicycle O.K., you cd swim, you think this rational shit is easy. I shd cry or scream you cd dance like a mutherfucka, excuse the language, who'm I talking to peaceful dignified spirit, you still know me don't you saying mother fucka to everything and trying to find something, spirit help me love me don't leave me.

The flower wasn't dying by the window when i screamed at your mother. They hadn't sung in the afternoon then. They hadn't gotten lost trying to find the cemetery. The other tale hadn't been told, the one about the cat with two wives who lost again hands down to his own grim life. You know that story.

I hadn't looked down at this dead girl then. With hands folded, and smile-pouting. Her lips stuck out more in death, not mad, but damn there was so much she hadn't done or seen, which makes the shallowness of life that angels blank on so much, finally you know the shit's not even worthy of pulsating perfection. Oh love.

But people stood outside in the rain waiting to get in to see this dead girl. And the priest chanted, and the people thought and felt and acted, some wept. Some demanded an investigation of death. Some wanted to sue. Some wrote poems. Some got drunk. Some fucked women in the dark then, not knowing you watched.

I looked at the newspaper. I took a walk. I thought about a lot of things. I wanted a story, a tale, to tell you. Something you could remember of me, and yrself, to take with you long journey; you were born on the 12th, the second fifth, the reach, at the fifth round, into new humanity. I'm at 7. A first knowing. The realizing, that when I die, if this is last I'll come no more to these shitty towns. This little girl that dances, don't be jealous of her spirit, she's in a box out somewhere in newjersey. Somebody's gonna build a bench nearby, out of stone. I might come out some late afternoons or mornings, very early, still wet and cold.

It's about love, yes it is. And about feeling, and who we are, who we really are alone joined up together with so many hearts to the beginning of the human epic. (I told you these people slid down the rock, plop, back to the one-celled, they thought it was hip, to be so positive.)

We'll be alone without you creative child. My youth. My tenderness. My warm creature with the big ass and lips. What we knew turns to dust, at this very moment. How fast you can travel. Baby. How much speed and jive with you, so much, so beautiful, I can't quite understand. What can I educate you to now, you know so much more than any body. You left it. The dumb part of what I remember. Not even a story. And I know this doesn't make sense.

No Body   No Place

The shapes in the darkness had histories. Falling out of windows failing to become mayor of their mothers' universes. We must work together, put on the right brightness. The clothes. Our robes and gowns. Stop killing each other, wheel to face the actual Killers.

I wanted to do this and wheel. And wheel. And wheel. And be. And couldn't. Monkees walked on my fingers. People misunderstood. In such a short space, to rise. To float. To be the other. Above the skin. Bones tossed, left. A will in the left of the desk, in a brown envelope. Do not dispute what is there. Of light and despair.

To keep from thinking, which is evil. Sky does not think. Nor trees. To stand at the edge of that feeling because I couldn't use it. Instead I'd be in Alabama with the fire. In the shadow thrown dancing by the cracker's ego. And them. They'd get their shit together and try to leave. They'd try to throw it all out. They'd try to start again. And grown children, who one day will be faced with the same prerogatives, the same alternatives. The same lies, and crisscross. Trying to grow. Trying to be good people. God people. God men, and Women of the earth and sky.

* * *

The telephone rings and it is a friend of mine. Who talks smoothly and softly about things I am interested in. To back and take away your yes from, your eyes from, the event. The torture and manhoodmaking. The final step with hands open, and eyes open, to embrace whatever. I could not get angry at the tortured. I could only hate myself. And love them beyond their knowledge, and they rise anyway. They reach anyway. They make their moves, as I make mine. But at the level of each his separate adjustment to being God. To being owners of all that there is.

* * *

Many years ago I wanted to be myself. And still I walk that same line. This man whose life I watched. Whose soul is mine, and another's. This child beaten for his love and his stupidity. In the earth fire wind of the era of our captivity. When we dressed like beasts and walked into enclaves of suffering like cowboys. Hair glued separately, identifying the part of the world we'd been oppressed in. Dirt and dust, and torn pants. And big eyes blacked and tossed dumbly to the ground, and held by our friends from the final killing and disappearance into the woods of life. Where the sweet fruit and inner adventure is. My lovely woman with me, in long green and softness. She stands there smiling, with me, now, forever, as something turns colors and sweetens the forest itself.

But in a stark black and white tube. With my brothers and sisters on benches for sale. And the beasts themselves darting in and out inside, in their capes and revenge. The machines. The rumbling insides of the robots. Inside her "chest" the motors whirr . . . "NUrse NURSE," the name she responds to, stumble-walking toward us, rotting Kate Smith, hands outstretched the mummy a missionary to help us, to cover us over with dirt, again, but we rise through, flowers, in bright colors, even trampled we rise and hug the sun and sky and are strong, believe me, strong.

My brother stands there beat and bleary eyes. His friends with him shambling, a rude group, a motion, a place in the universe. "We demand to be loved. We demand to be alive. We demand to be looked at like human beings. We demand that we are always so beautiful. And dirty. And bent. And drunk. And ignorant. And praying to mover of universe. To the east or the west or the south or the north or the pointless no place in space world of loves and adventure. All place are us and God, and we demand in the death shadow of the yellowow world, something for ourselves. Our friend here is hurt. Is injured. Help him, lady."

And he stands there with his opening of the sweater, and his droopy pants, and shows the stab wounds. The blood and tearing gap. His heart just beneath it, throwing the blood to the top.

* * *

in the sticks in the sticks in the flying thin money for somebody dirt a lot of us lived together through this. You read the newspapers? Have you seen that statue of Lincoln? How it's turned green? You walk down there near the jew with the busted head. In the army navy store. And the pimps in sam johnson hoods bending so cool. Fulla punks of the universe in exactly the same order as we.

There were the neighbors and whoever lived here. With us. Whoever passed through in sinister laments. Pointing the shadows, conducting their own adventures. They'd hurt, and look in the mirrors of our silence with big shoes, stomping the music book a blue stamp a final agony for the soul gone weak in the seas.

He was a man who'd glued himself to that life. His hat, and rolly girth, a speech like that, and himself flying toward a basket, not sure of the shot, but the power was definitely hip. We are the zigzags of our own design. Is it secret? Are they walking the streets each night with hands in their pockets to see God? Or what? I mean why are we here, if you don't know, sit down, be calm, zippppppppp.

I couldn't be but sitting here seeing and hearing. Like phones and pointed grimaces, white dudes answering the no for our lives. I couldn't walk stupid or unfeeling or in hip germany, forever. It was my own life. I looked at it. Watched it in other people's eyes. It was nothing to me but real.

So what can I say to remember? The smooth thing, you think you want. You want to label me. Describe me finally for an elk.? "Why yes, you fool."

* * *

I saw (that) man. The drifts of his life. In sequence. A dance a masquerade of effects who which were will who plys the place, moving. Exact any trip. Back. Exact any trip. The same. And no fooling no lying to the lord the god of ooooooooooo his own foreverforce . . .

I thought I was talking to a schoolteacher and wanted to explain something for him to teach. When someone asks me to react. When I do. It's not for real. It's lower than that. Tilted somehow, black people. I know what I want to see, am the only one . . . but he passed, he passed. he's slow his taught his is a moving being of the one thought the one the one.

This is an exact crevice. This is a sunrise like seeing the logic of the white castle. The hamburgers and gauze hats and little cups of coffee and orange drink. the slavery. I know these girls want something to fill them up. they can't long so need so much leap out of themselves to grab at the essence of life. They are always.

The gas talks. Water, solids. Animals. Understand the total meaning of the world. Understand what men are for. What they will be. If he could crawl up the street waving his arms and drunk with the idea of loss, drag himself up, and think about the giants he warred against, and and what and crack it, oh god what have i done?

This is the silhouette of the man. The flashes of light. Signals from the future evolutions, the future worlds that we will be there. What we make and are, we long for our strength, as a completion of the energy we project.

Now and Then

This musician and his brother always talked about spirits. They were good musicians, talking about spirits, and they had them, the spirits, and soared with them, when they played. The music would climb, and bombard everything, destroying whole civilizations, it seemed. And then I suppose, while they played, whole civilizations actually *were* destroyed. Leveled. The nuns whimpered with church spears through their heads. Blind blond babies bled and bled. Dogs ate their mothers and television was extinct except the image burned in it forever, in the future soft museums of our surviving civilization. A black way. A black life. From the ways and roads of the black man living, surviving, being strong.

But when they stopped, the brothers, they were not that strong. Like any of us, the music, their perfection, was their perfect projection of themselves, past any bullshit walking around tied up unspiritual shit. They could be caught with white girls, and talk unintelligibly, or sometimes around one's glasses a little sliver of white fear would idle, and he'd laugh it away, and talk about his music, shadowboxing, practicing his survival and perfection.

Mostly their peters slammed them, and brought them lower than themselves, or the need to live, like to have money, and be whole in the tincan halfassed sense the white man's way, which he put on us, and is still so much a part of all our lives. (A man on the radio explaining black-power.)

I mean they could only talk when they were not playing. As I can only talk, or feel the frustration of needing too. Of not sitting in the circle of circumscribed light. Reeling. Passing. (Like my dead lovely girl, passed, passed, passed, gone.) Getting into the next level of vision. Seeing and being. I want to go. I want to fly. Lift me spirit. Help me. Just talk. That's all. With the tongue in the roof of my mouth. Just spirit. Nothing but. I hurt. I want. I need. All these endless flesh frustration categories. Which are only that. This is a saint. No place. This is a god. No where. This is a feeling. Me. I am all feeling. Here by the wet window burned in its tone. I am all the not being that my limit has set, not knowing yet my whole. Yet I do and can not speak with my entire spirit. Can not fly. Though I understand the need. The way. I do not can not be do are. Walls. Walls. Lie in the death of the almighty. Wishing.

Like I write to keep from talking, and try by that to see clear to where I must go. Chakra. Enlightenment.

The seven lives. The many planetary adventures. Air fire water. Scale. Hung in the balance to see the deaths. Tell them horns. Tell them words. Tell them example of a man little man with big eyes went away came back grew loved made things died without point, in the history of no world and the world passed, the continent sank, and nothing but nothing was ever accomplished since everything was already done, and what more could be done.

The brothers cast shadows in the world, and tales were told about them. They told tales about themselves. One was short and one was tall. They scared a lot of people because they were new. They *were* spiritual. But not like Norman. Black Norman short brother brought to my house one afternoon, he was looking like the passer, like he knew more than any of us. "You think it's about personalities." He said that. "About personalities," and the door swung open sunlight, no, nothing, came in, to the force of, to the heart of, my self. I cdn't speak. You think it's about personalities. You think it's about your self. Whew. was in the air. I see him years later standing in a doorway on 125th street, the ways of men. Further out, gone, than any of us. Even now, with the wind of God blows through me. "Come on faggot," his face turned on 130th street in that stance of hard ashy elbows, and read the deep cowardice of a wd be killer. All of the would be killers, cowards, and dancers with high fists, killing the village white killers. And the killer, JM, the soldier, subsided. To darkness of more fears, and another road he had to find, having seen the fire in Black Norman rage into heavens we know nothing of.

Black Norman was not always Black Norman either. He was weaker too. He was not always in the rain on the street in the doorway communing with God. He wanted money. He wanted his flesh. He *thought* he was strong sometimes (though in his weakest moments). God of Norman of God of where I touch. Feel this, and pass. All you dudes. Feel this, and pass.

But they, the brothers were pals of mine. Good friends, in a world of alligators and shitheads, lunatics, happy liars, cowards, white people. There was warmth. There was something done, in our inch. But God knows. God chooses whom he will. (Your prerogative, ol man, to call such, knowing the blue eyes of the will, of the days, of the number passing, all, such, and me, and the . . . heart stopped, girl, please, I want to know, where's the door I came in yestiddy, where??? I cdn't, don't, and they look at me, I want . . . stop it, stoooopidt!)

My pals and me, against everything. It seemed. They made music like heaven's bowels. I loved them in the sound. They loved women tho. Like Amos and Andy in the Harem of the Butchers. It was a conquest they thought about winning shit. Like boys. The tall one was all boy, a kid, really. Raw, like they say, of new kinda gunfighters type. The other rooted in a cleaner rhythm than the world around him, though he created the things that could weaken him. Responded. There are invisible allegiances in our bones. Things we must look at. Why? The smoke of smells. The web of things we've touched or seen. Womb-earth.

People can be corny at the same time they're not. Can reach that? (Children line up against the wall and select your failure machine. He's going down, wind, scarf badarf waves, hello clancey jackson sits on the steps looking at the girl, can grow, the g clef vibrates hairs pussies, conglomerates of afternoon triumphs, evening walks across the floor, as beautiful. They want to be Gods. We must desire god and his ism.

(I can describe one guy tall with a large adam's apple. With wirerim glasses and sneaky smile. Sneaky high up there, pardner? Har to breaf???

The other more flash gordon without the popsicle. Maybe a joint sometime. Whenever. And a white tuft of sparks thrust out his lower jaw.

This is the scandal of a small town that all the stupid people are the same as in a big town, so they seem stupider. Dig?? So the lovers, seem, S-O-M-E-H-O-W, loveier (is that a category of human espresso??)

Sometimes they looked like Batgroup unemployed. No place, like, to hover. (In all honesty, this is a one-way street, come back, the shit's changed. Evolver,

which is different from revolver, which has long hair
and kills. Even in song.)

"Black People We Must Take Over This Planet As
The Prime Possessors Of Natural Energies." Red Hook
always wanted them to write a song with that as the
title, but they didn't when I was "knowin'dem" (a de-
scription of bat-street, in back of the sixteenth dead
president, in bronze and the key to the city in the future brain of the tall basketball players dodging father
divine's hustlers on the street. You cannot ask for more
than immaculation????? (I cdn't wish no worse on you.)
Except we need each other. Red Hook would lecture like
Sun-Ra sometimes, when Ra is talking to certain corny
niggers about selling out black people. Batgroup would
leave for the midwest at night, zooming, and blowing,
and come back hooked up, literate, in dey shit, fresh.

Or trailing chicks around, they'd go get the energy
to do that. Here. One's wife was somewhere and somewhere else. One was a pole. Like wood. Wresting a
killer humility. A egogod, telling the shadow of what
you claim you never had. Or left, the older ones claim to
have gained knowledge through error. And how much
of that is really true? Guess?? And they'd follow, or
one would, Red Hook, or the source. Maybe rubbed on
Hook's coat or African shirt. A dazzle, a stink glow of the
source, the possibility of being kings and loved men of
a strong people.

They wanted a show. A place. It was good and bad. There too was too much slack for bad wind. They schemed, and darted. Made shit, and you think, didn't realize it? Think about yrself. You do the same shit. People watch. They watch from across the street through the window with their linoleums drying in late afternoons. They chart your life. They know you walk on glass splinters running shit, like on the radio. Murray the K type shit. "We've all seen what you can do, man." JB talking.

So they'd make both scenes like on a bridge, going to Europe with the Snowmen, then coming back with the key to the invasion of the warm countries by the barbarians, the coldbeasts. And snuggled up with one, a lady, MY God WHAT WOULD THEY TELL THEM BITCHES LOCKED UP IN COPENHAGEN? WITH ICE BLOWING AGAINST THE WINDOWS. AND SOME SHIT HAPPENING IN NEW YORK OR CLEVELAND DIDN'T INVOLVE YOU? YOU DIDN'T KNOW??? WHAT??? and come back to Atomic Bomb shit.

"You shure yo' shit strong enough, my man??"

Ornette in a hindu Edwardian sack of jewish bass stealers.

But it is in an age of The Miracles. Which must be put to work for us. All our energy. Even the brothers must finally be used for the lot. To raise u. To fly us all into the grace we seek. Which is, without light what they mean then by, Power. Amen.

The night I want to talk about they had gone to this girl's house I know. (She was sort of an unofficial city limit hostess in them parts. And she had a sickness then, covered people, turn them into different parts of a whole. You want I should characterize that whole? You want I shd patch my wings or retreat to the cellar to brood? It was spread so clean and cool tight got mucho everything-o actually, everybody had some of the shit inem. People stood around. Music was playing. Slick thin insect pee pees were uncovered. Screens full of air. And the aspirations of all the neighbors, in that particular part of the earth, they had rent to pay, get up next day for hip jobs, meet head on with the white unicorn unfortunately being ignorant and blowing bugles on the top of the baptist churches (UNCONSCIOUSLY, MOTHERFUCKER, ALRIGHT!!!???) to warn Cary Grant's boys that eastboots were about to slay them.

Is this the scene yr *avant-garde* shit degravitates?? Inhabitates?? Ya Wohl, marches out the plank splashes into the little rich lady section of universal attention. A vibration in the yellow pages. Pussy for sale!

Aww crisscross shit. Crisscross shiiiiiit, yeh. Reall crisscross shit. People opening and closing doors. Telephones. Creep business being done. Yeh. Singing chicks. Chick wd stand there like some mediocre white lady with one-strap gown and janis paige button and lion eatin her ass, really swingingk.)

The husband was calling for the muslim woman. She was devout and weird to the poorer americans. "ALLAH WAS VERY HIP." That's a photomontage of success. "Yesh I was righteous before Bud or Elijah." Meanwhile, there is a trumpet player fuggingkher. He's hip. He's a spiritual beingk. He's spooky. He knows about ghoses. He's a strongbean like John Carradine of duh good guise. He's fuggingkher, riley, really. You goddam catholic pay attention to the meter!

"You mean . . . What . . . naw . . . really no kidding. Really?"

Yeh it's the tall brother . . . yeh, goes in the room with the broad, then she gets a call from whatsaname, the hostess, that this muslim dude is comin. Like her husbain. Yeh.

Was he playing earlier that evening . . . tall brother? (Nobody here to ask, children playing in the streets. Gentle movement of the earth.) But anyway around that same time he walked water legends with his sound and grew into something he'd never be except in that thrust of his own invisible energy.

Chick hears this and panics. Everybody in the joint did. Hostess. Lil brother. Lil bro's woman, who's really pinhead priest's chick, stopped making it with funkybutt the organiz for a minute, took up with higher math cats. Maybe bealbelly the mystic ex-photographer saxophone player who has speakers inserted in the stones. They blah. They blah. They blah.

Cat comes in finally, the muslim. Tall brother splits to the bedroom lays on the bed under the cover, stiff as wood pole. (Remember I described him befoe??) Hostess pins him almost faints. Muslim chick, OPuretwat the black beauty, pulls it all off, except for a second she fades into the bedroom for a suck off a burning joint. Frozen for a second, in tableau,

the shit is run successfully
muslim chick and her husband
leave

another frozen moment (EXCEPT THE RUSH OF ALL THINGS IS THE RUSH OF ALL THINGS AND ON IS STILL EVER WAS AND IS NOW OM-MMMMMMMMMMMMMMMMMMMMMMMMM THE ENDLESS)

Then everybody unfreezes and a loud cackle of success in America rises up from this not really humble abode. Lil brother is happy, and puts on his newest record. Hostess titters walks around touching her guests on the arm. Tall brother finally comes out of the bedroom sez, "Shit, that cat cdn't seen me anyway, even if he'd come in there. I was really a ghost."

Exactly before the laughter.

Answers in Progress

Can you die in airraid jiggle
torn arms flung through candystores
Touch the edge of answer. The waves of nausea
as change sweeps the frame of breath and meat.

"Stick a knife through his throat,"
he slid
in the blood
got up running toward
the blind newsdealer. He screamed
about "Cassius Clay," and slain there in the
street, the whipped figure of jesus, head opened
eyes flailing against his nose. They beat him to
pulpy answers. We wrote Muhammad Ali across his
face and chest, like a newspaper of bleeding meat.

The next day the spaceships landed. Art Blakey records
was what they were looking for. We gave them Butter-
corn Lady and they threw it back at us. They wanted
to know what happened to The Jazz Messengers. And
right in the middle, playing the Sun-Ra tape, the blanks
staggered out of the department store. Omar had missed
finishing the job, and they staggered out, falling in the
snow, red all over the face chest, the stab wounds in
one in the top of a Adam hat.

The space men thought that's what was really happening. One beeped (Ali mentioned this in the newspapers) that this was evolution. Could we dig it? Shit, yeh. We were laughing. Some blanks rounded one corner, Yaa and Dodua were behind them, to take them to the Center. Nationalized on the spot.

The space men could dig everything. They wanted to take one of us to a spot and lay for a minute, to dig what they were in to. Their culture and shit. Whistles Newark was broke up in one section. The dead mayor and other wops carried by in black trucks. Wingo, Rodney and them waving at us. They stopped the first truck and Cyril wanted to know about them thin cats hopping around us. He's always very fast finger.

Space men wanted to know what happened after Blakey. They'd watched but couldn't get close enough to dig exactly what was happening. Albert Ayler they dug immediately from Russell's mouth imitation. That's later. Red spam cans in their throats with the voices, and one of them started to scat. It wigged me. Bamberger's burning down, dead blancos all over and a cat from Sigma Veda, and his brothers, hopping up and down asking us what was happening.

We left Rachel and Lefty there to keep explaining. Me and Pinball had to go back to headquarters, and report Market Street Broad Street rundown. But we told them we'd talk to them. I swear one of those cats had a hip walk. Even thought they was hoppin and bop-adoppin up and down, like they had to pee. Still this one cat had a stiff tentacle, when he walked. Yeh; long blue winggly cats, with soft liquid sounds out of their throats for voices. Like, "You know where Art Blakey, Buhainia, is working?" We fell out.

* * *

Walk through life
beautiful more than anything
stand in the sunlight
walk through life
love all the things
that make you strong, be lovers, be anything
for all the people of
earth.

You have brothers
you love each other, change up
and look at the world
now, it's
ours, take it slow
we've long time, a long way
to go,

we have

each other, and the
world,
dont be sorry
walk on out through sunlight life, and know
we're on the go
for love
to open
our lives
to walk
tasting the sunshine
of life.

Boulevards played songs like that and we rounded up blanks where we had to. Space men were on the south side laying in some of the open houses. Some brothers came in from the west, Chicago, they had a bad thing going out there. Fires were still high as the buildings, but Ram sent a couple of them out to us, to dig what was happening. One of them we sent to the blue cats, to take that message, back. Could W dig what was happening with them? We sent our own evaluation back, and when I finished the report me and Pinball started weaving through the dead cars and furniture. Waving at the brothers, listening to the sounds, we had piped through the streets.

Smokey Robinson was on now. But straight up fast and winging. No more unrequited love. Damn Smokey got his thing together too. No more tracks or mirages. Just the beauty of the whole. I hope they play Sun-Ra for them blue cats, so they can dig where we at.

Magic City played later. By time we got to the courthouse. The whole top of that was out. Like you could look inside from fourth or fifth floor of the Hall of Records. Cats were all over that joint. Ogun wanted the records intact.

Past the playgrounds and all them blanks in the cold standing out there or laying on the ground crying. The rich ones really were funny. This ol cat me an Pinball recognized still had a fag thing going for him. In a fur coat, he was some kind of magistrate. Bobby and Moosie were questioning him about some silver he was supposed to have stashed. He was a silver freak. The dude was actually weeping. Crying big sobs; the women crowded away from him. I guess they really couldn't feel sorry for him because he was crying about money.

By the time we got to Weequahic Avenue where the space men and out-of-town brothers were laying I was tired as a dog. We went in there and wanted to smoke some bush, but these blue dudes had something better. Taste like carrots. It was a cool that took you. You thought something was mildly amusing and everything seemed interesting.

I talked with Pinball and the blue leader about Ben Caldwell's paintings . . . the one where the guy is smoking the reefer. We thought about the changing reference, of our new world. As it stood already in the old ruins. And we all felt like Bird. The old altosax-ophonist . . . but the limits opened out into the pure lyric tone of powerful beings. But when the Sun-Ra tape came on this blue dude really opened up. He dug the hell out of it. Perfect harmony these cats had too. Boooooo—Iiiiiiiiiooooooooooooooo . . . daaaaa ahhhh-hhhh aaaaahhhhhh . . . booooo OOOOOOOOOOOOO oooooooooaaaaaaaaaoooaaaaa

Claude McKay I started quoting. Four o'clock in the morning to a blue dude gettin cooled out on carrots. We didn't have no duty until ten o'clock the next day, and me and Lorenzo and Ish had to question a bunch of prisoners and stuff for the TV news. Chazee had a play to put on that next afternoon about the Chicago stuff. Ray talked to him. And the name of the play was Big Fat Fire.

Man I was tired. We had taped the Sigma. They were already infested with Buddhas there, and we spoke very quietly about how we knew it was our turn. I had burned my hand somewhere and this blue cat looked at it hard and cooled it out. White came in with the design for a flag he'd been working on. Black heads, black hearts, and blue fiery space in the background. Love was heavy in the atmosphere. Ball wanted to know what the blue chicks looked like. But I didn't. Cause I knew after tomorrow's duty, I had a day off, and I knew somebody waitin for me at my house, and some kids, and some fried fish, and those carrots, and wow.

That's the way the fifth day ended.

March 1967

Also by Amiri Baraka/LeRoi Jones and available from Akashic Books

BLACK MUSIC

256 pages, trade paperback reissue, $16.95
The sequel to Amiri Baraka's seminal work of music criticism, *Blues People*. Featuring a new introduction by the author and an interview by Calvin Reid.

"Jones has learned—and this has been very rare in jazz criticism—to write about music as an artist." —Nat Hentoff

THE SYSTEM OF DANTE'S HELL

160 pages, trade paperback reissue, $15.95
A remarkable 1965 novel of childhood and youth, spiraling out of Dante's *Inferno*. Featuring a new introduction by Woodie King Jr.

"Much of the novel is an expression of the intellectual and moral lost motion of the age . . . the special agony of the American Negro." —*New York Times Book Review*

HOME: SOCIAL ESSAYS

288 pages, trade paperback reissue, $15.95
A seminal Jones/Baraka literary land mine, featuring a new introduction by the author.

"Jones/Baraka usually speaks as a Negro—and always as an American. He is eloquent, he is bold. He demands rights—not conditional favors." —*New York Times Book Review*

TALES OF THE OUT & THE GONE

200 pages, trade paperback original, $16.95
Short Stories. An *Essence* magazine best seller.

"In his prose as in his poetry, Baraka is at his best a lyrical prophet of despair who transfigures his contentious racial and political views into a transcendent, 'outtelligent' clarity." —*New York Times Book Review* (Editors' Choice)